May 2020

D0464067

Kansas City, MO Public Library
00001877726005

Rae Earl

MY LIFE GONE VIRAL

[Imprint]
MAKE YOUR MARK

New York

To Kevin & Katherine
9–5 vegetable kind of people
With thanks for The Land
of Lost Content

[Imprint]
MAKE YOUR MARK

A part of Macmillan Publishing Group, LLC
120 Broadway, New York, NY 10271

MY LIFE GONE VIRAL. Copyright © 2020 by Rae Earl. All rights reserved.
Printed in the United States of America.

Library of Congress Control Number: 2019941062

ISBN 978-1-250-13380-9 (hardcover) / ISBN 978-1-250-13381-6 (ebook)

Our books may be purchased in bulk for promotional, educational, or business use.
Please contact your local bookseller or the Macmillan Corporate and Premium Sales Department at
(800) 221-7945 ext. 5442 or by email at MacmillanSpecialMarkets@macmillan.com.

Book design by Ellen Duda and Carolyn Bull

Imprint logo designed by Amanda Spielman

First edition, 2020

10 9 8 7 6 5 4 3 2 1

fiercereads.com

Don't illegally download this book
If you do, this is my curse
You'll find big spiders in your sink
And holes in your purse

Cents and dollars will tumble out
Without you being aware,
There'll be flies in your coffee
And bubble gum in your hair

#FelineFash

It was the hot dog that did it. Definitely.

Generally, you can't have your cat wearing something made of pork on its head without people asking some serious questions about your life. If *your* pet has ever worn your lunch, you'll know what I mean. It's a game changer.

The thing is, eating is difficult when you're thinking hard. You just trust your body to do its chewy thing. The problem was my jaw had kind of skipped after my brain and checked into Hotel La-La Land. My mouth and eyes really didn't notice that an entire frankfurter had somersaulted from a bun. I just kept chomping on the carbs, staring into space whilst my cat did a runway show into the kitchen with some seriously avant-garde headgear.

I only noticed when Mum said, "Millie. Dave is modeling your dinner. Any thoughts?"

Then she gave one of her "all-seeing oracle" parental looks. You know the sort of thing. The "I know you're worried about something but you're not telling me because you're too worried and now *I'm* worried and basically THIS IS A GLOBAL WORRY PANDEMIC" kind of looks.

My mum can tell a lot from a half-a-second stare. It's her special talent. Face reading, guilt-tripping, and getting things out of you that you don't want to talk about. I think the FBI needs her. She'd crack anyone in minutes.

I tried to get her off my case by asking her if she'd managed to get her phone out and record Dave doing her thing for a vlog but Mum said, "No. Creating great content is of no concern to me. It's even less of a concern to me when I think my little girl might be working herself up into a state about things."

There was another epic "drill into my brain" gaze, but at that point Dave sashayed back into the room with a sausage behind her. Mum was distracted, mainly because Dave looked like she should be on the cover of *Vogue*. You've never seen a cat work it with such total conviction. She was Gigi Hadid, but with a tail and a flea collar.

I took my chance then. "I need to go and get my stuff from Dad's place," I snapped very quickly. That's your only hope in a situation like this. Deflecting.

Mum kept looking at Dave, but said firmly, "Okay, Millie, but when you come back we need an honest chat. Anxiety doesn't just steal sausages. It's a thief of your time and your happiness. And it's something . . ."

At that moment Dave jumped onto my lap and dropped a gherkin into my palm. I didn't know I'd lost that, either.

Yes, Mum. We can have a chat. I just need to get things straight in MY head first. And that may take a while. In fact, it may take forever.

But I didn't say that to her. I just gave her a hug, threw Dave the rest of my hot dog bun, and left. Dave loves buns. We call bread "sliced cat-bohydrate" in our house.

I've just realized I'm still holding the gherkin. Random sliced gherkins in your hand usually mean something is not quite right with the world. Let me try to explain what. I don't think it makes me sound very nice, but it's the truth.

#lifefacts

When I'm on my own and walking I can think. My feet are smarter than my jaw; they can do their job really well without me worrying about them. When people ask me what my favorite part of my body is I ALWAYS say my legs. It's not how they look (quite skinny calves, BIG thighs, freaky tall toes I've inherited from Dad), it's what they do.

My brain needs some love, you can tell. It's like when you accidentally leave your glass underneath the Coke dispenser and then you get distracted by a cute dog outside (don't tell Dave). You look around and, all of a sudden, you're creating a mini Niagara Falls. I'm like that. I'm overflowing with everything.

Mum, who has a head like mine, says at times when you feel like your brain is about to burst, write down the facts. Not the things you *think* might happen. JUST the facts. You don't need a laptop, a phone, or a pen. You doodle it all down in your head.

- I'm moving back in with my mum and her neat freak boyfriend, Gary. I moved out a few months ago because he made my life impossible, as he wants to ban dust and grime globally. Also, my mum can be a dictator. A benevolent and low-level one, but she still has some power-hungry tendencies. However, NOW we've agreed to compromise. I will try to keep my room clean (well, clean-ISH), stop making epic biscuit crumb bombs (Gary's description, NOT mine) and stop Dave from surfing on Gary's robot vacuum cleaner (impossible. Dave is a speed freak, a celebrity stunt cat, and fears no one and nothing—not even surprise frankfurters). I'm looking forward to it. I've missed my mum. YES, she's too strict, but she's basically a feminist warrior with epic taste in ankle boots. Don't get me wrong, I've loved living with my dad, Granddad, and Aunty Teresa. It's been great getting to know Dad a bit more. He's been in other countries for a lot of my life, and I do feel like I've missed out. Aunty Teresa has also been living abroad in a way—just in her head on her own planet. I think Granddad has really enjoyed having me around. He may be an epic sexist stuck in the last century, but he appreciates my streak of sensible. I love all of them, but I'd like to be in a house with an actual lock on the front door that works. It's also difficult to watch TV when two people in their forties are having a danceoff to Bruno Mars. I just want more . . . *order.* Yes, I'm tragic. I like things on the quiet side and it's difficult to get peace when Aunty Teresa's fixer-upper ice cream truck is playing "Pop Goes the Weasel" in the front yard. Also, my dresser is an exercise bike that no one uses. So, yes, I'd like something a bit more . . . normal. I will miss them, though. It's good to know some adults stay a bit silly and don't think that having a clean kitchen sink is the peak of their existence. Gary's permanent aftershave is a mixture of Versace for Men and white vinegar.

- I have a boyfriend. Danny. It took a while for us to get together. I was confused or he was. We BOTH were, I guess. It all got a bit weird BUT now we are an official trademarked item. He's funny, kind, and completely owns his own brand of Canadian handsomeness. He also has a pencil case in the shape of a llama and he doesn't care what anyone thinks. Nothing ever seems to faze him. He's permanently chill—like a gorgeous refrigerator but with warm arms. In the past few weeks he's been incredible because honestly, with everything that's been going on, things have been stressful. Danny is phenomenal at just making things seem manageable. He's an accidental life coach. You give him a mountain and he makes it feel like a tiny hill (in the good way). I've really appreciated that AND I am NOT being a pathetic girl. I've just needed good friends who make me laugh—and he does. He's also an epic kisser. Yeah, Danny is almost perfect. Except for liking noodles with too much garlic, but I've learned to live with that. Extra-strong mints are our friend.

This is the hard one. I'll just try to say it quickly.
I can't say it quickly. Who am I kidding? This is BIG.

- I went viral. Well, me and Dave the cat went viral. She went crazy behind me when I was doing a really personal vlog and now we've got real human followers and someone who manages "life content creators" (why do these people always use fancy names?) wants to meet me to discuss how she can help me become "even bigger." Lauren, my BFF, thinks this is wonderful. Erin, previously known as Lady Uber Cool who was sensationally outed as the person behind the most EVIL Instagram account EVER, suddenly wants to be besties with me. My granddad is a tiny bit impressed even though he has no idea what it all means. I was just another rando recording videos in a shed and now, because of a bizarre feline accident, I'm big. And it's what I want. I'm viral and I want to keep being viral. Mum gets it. She says this is AMBITION and an acknowledgment of my innate skill set and I should EMBRACE it. I want to be a success. It is FINE to say that. Viral. It's everything I wanted and it's EVERYTHING I want but now that it's happened . . .

I'll be really honest with you. It's all got a bit intense. The truth is, I'm having trouble coping with this whole "being quite great all the time" thing.

What I've found out is that I can cope with being useless. That sounds insane, I KNOW, but it's sort of fine to me. Even dreadful, crushing defeat and "throw my lunch all over the cafeteria whilst everyone watches and then applauds" mistakes. I just go to my special Zen Loo cubicle for five minutes, take some deep breaths, and start again. But success? Success is HARD. I now understand why celebrities do wild stuff when they get even a tiny bit famous. It's ODD when people you don't know like you. The whole world is applauding you and telling you you're brilliant, but inside you don't feel any different to how you felt a week ago. You just want to say "Dear World. I'm still the same Millie. I haven't got a clue what I'm doing and I don't know what I'm going to do next either and what if it all goes wrong and . . ."

I'm taking deep breaths. HUGE ones. Mum told me she used to be this way. It's anxiety. She learned to manage it. So can I.

I know what you're thinking, because I'd be thinking the same. Millie, shouldn't you be in Vegas with a massive billboard and lots of backup dancers in sequined leotards? Because YOU have become a diva with a capital D in big lights. What a brat. What's up with me?! It's like when people post a selfie of themselves crying. Liam Whitehead did one when his skateboard lost its wheel. It's good to see a guy comfortable with his full-on emotions, but we felt total sympathy for him anyway! We didn't need a photo of his big red face with a filter that made him look like a really angry opossum with conjunctivitis.

Like Liam's crazy eye, this is probably something I shouldn't share with anyone because everyone will just start screaming STOP BEING AN ATTENTION SEEKER!

I KNOW this situation is wonderful. THIS IS ACTUALLY ALL A DREAM. If this were a film, I just would have run off to a massive piece of music, all smiles after a big Danny kiss, epic filter, skin LUMINOUS, probably riding a unicorn.

But this is real life and I'm waiting for disaster. In *my* sort of movie I'm the person shouting on the beach that the tsunami is heading straight for us. Everyone else ignores me and carries on sunbathing and eating fries.

And when the tsunami finally arrives, it's just a tiny wave that knocks over one beach parasol and slightly splashes a lifeguard.

I need to sort myself out. And fast. What I'm doing isn't wrong. Influencers need to be sure of themselves. It's feminist to go after what you want. It's basically being Beyoncé and she can do no wrong. At times like this, I need my Jay-Z.

#WearATree

Danny's mum likes me. I can tell. When she opens the front door she basically drags me in and smiles from ear to ear. "Oh! Here she is! The acceptable face of cat lady!" she shouts. I think Mrs. Trudeau is also relieved, as Danny's last serious girlfriend was mainly mascara-based and there's only so long you can talk about lash length. "Millie!" she whispers. "He's upstairs! Tell him that he needs to pack SOMETHING. He can't JUST wear branches. However much he'd like to."

This makes no sense, but the Trudeau household often doesn't. It's a bit out there.

When I get to Danny's room he's looking at an empty bag.

"Hello, Mills! What do you pack for a holistic spa weekend? I'm thinking hardly anything. I might just wear foliage!"

I stare at him. "Yeah, your mum is worried about that. I don't think branches will work for you. When are you going?"

Danny looks at me with a slightly folded-up face. "Er. Tomorrow. Did I not mention it?"

"No, you didn't," I say casually. My mouth is casual. In my brain, I

am not casual in any way. I am annoyed. This is Danny. I love that he's
so relaxed, but sometimes this means he lives in an extreme chill bubble.
He forgets to tell me key details about his life. It's not that he doesn't
care, he just floats around the earth a lot. It's Aunty Teresa disease—just
a less severe case.

Danny puts his arm around me. "You're annoyed," he says. "I can
tell."

Danny isn't intimidated by strong women, so I serve it up in a brilliant but not hysterical way.

"It *would* be nice to know where you are going to be. I do actually
like spending some time with you. I'm not being overdramatic. I just
love having a laugh with you. And you get the vlog thing even though
you don't really get the vlog thing."

Danny isn't really into social media. He can check his phone twice a
day and not be completely itchy about it.

"Sorry, Mills." Danny sighs. "Fair enough. Now, do you think I can
just get away with a handful of leaves and some mud?"

He says this with a wink. He makes me laugh a lot. However, at
times like this, I can feel my no-nonsense mum invading my brain and
it's fantastic.

"I'm not organizing your wardrobe for you. Pay me to be your stylist
and I'll help. Until then you're on your own."

"Anyway," I say, "I've got to go and see my family."

Danny hugs me very hard and we have a superb kiss. We have per-
fected this. We're A-list kissers. "Have a great weekend!" he whispers.
"Be you. Be brilliant and go for it. Do a fantastic vlog about bad boy-
friends who don't tell their partners where they are going. That'll go

viral. Actually, don't do that. I'd rather keep out of it, really. BUT GO VIRAL! Whatever, just BE YOU."

This is why Danny and I work. He gets me and he gives me an ego turbo-boost. I sort of skip all the way to Granddad's house. It's not exactly a skip, as that would be highly embarrassing as I'm not actually seven, but it's a very positive stompy walk.

#CallTeresa

When I get to Granddad's house, Aunty Teresa answers the door. I ask her what she is doing. Rule number one for a calm life: NEVER ask Aunty Teresa what she is doing.

"Ermm. We are mostly doing goat noises and listing people we'd like on our dartboard of hate," she says, like it's the most totally normal thing in the world.

"And how does that work?" I ask. I never learn. Rule number two: Don't ask for details.

Aunty Teresa drags me into the front room. My dad is there standing over a homemade target, which has a big red bull's-eye marked THE WORST in the middle of it. He gives me a huge hug.

"Millie," he says proudly, "behold the greatest advance in stress relief ever! You simply pin all the things you can't stand onto this, and then you throw darts at it."

I read what Aunty Teresa and Dad have written on it.

- Noisy eaters
- People who post a sad face on Facebook so everyone writes "Are you okay, Hun?"—JUST TELL US WHAT IS ACTUALLY WRONG!

- People who walk slowly in the mall. I'm shopping. MOVE!
- Seahorses

"What's up with seahorses?" I ask.

Aunty Teresa looks at me like I've asked something incredibly stupid. "Well, you can't ride them, and all they do is float around looking pretty. I want more from my marine creatures. Look at sharks! They bring DRAMA!"

"But male seahorses can give birth!" I tell her. I've been googling a lot. Lauren and I have fact wars. This is mainly because Lauren thinks she can go on game shows with all her knowledge and become very rich very quickly. For her, the weirder the fact the better. The bizarre thing is, trivia also really helps me manage my stress. When my brain is worrying what the capital of Bhutan is, it's not full of anxiety about other stuff I can't control.

"Pregnant fish men! Fake news!" Teresa says. And I have to google this fact to prove it to her. She makes her "massively amazed" face where her nose accordions into her forehead and she practically dislocates her skull. "Right," she shouts, "seahorses are off and goats are back on."

My dad looks outraged and hollers, "NO! Think of the cheese!"

Aunty Teresa pounces on him and they start wrestling on the floor. They don't notice as I leave for the kitchen. Granddad is standing there mopping the floor. He seems like he's in another world. I say "Hi" to him, but he just carries on cleaning. I wave madly in his direction. When he's tuned out, this is the only thing that ever works.

"Oh, hello, superstar," he finally says. He's called me "superstar" since all this going-viral stuff happened. I don't really like it, but this is Granddad trying to be sweet. He doesn't normally believe in compliments. He thinks they make you arrogant and according to him there are few things worse than a "big-headed female." Yes, he is sexist as he's ancient and most people were back then. Women used to be sexist to themselves! I make allowances for my grandpa. He's family.

"Sorry, Millie," he says, "I was in a world of my own. I do my best thinking when I'm mopping. Once you are used to the nature of the job, your body does one thing and it frees your mind to ponder the complexities of the universe."

I give Granddad a cuddle. We are beyond words sometimes, especially when he goes too deep.

"I expect you've come around to get your things. So you're leaving me with these two fools?"

At that point I hear Teresa yell, "PUT MUSHROOMS BACK ON THE DARTBOARD OF HATE. They are EVIL. It's like eating moldy mini umbrellas."

Granddad looks at me sadly. "I'll miss you, gal. I will miss you."

We have an uncomfortable moment. This is because Granddad doesn't really do feelings. He gets emotional and then changes the subject to the first thing that pops into his head before you have a chance to react.

"Nothing wrong with mushrooms!" he shouts at Teresa. "Well, except the ones that can kill you."

He looks at me and winks. "Would you like to use my shed for one of your things before you go? For old times' sake?"

I've been using Granddad's shed as my vlog spot. I'd sort of hoped he'd let me keep on using it, but I think he wants his man cave back and, as I hear Teresa and my dad fighting over murder fungi, I kind of understand that. It's good to have a place to hide in life.

I put my arm around Granddad's shoulder and give him a kiss. He grabs his mop and pretends to attack me with it. That's one of the ways he tells me he loves me.

Families are weird, aren't they? All families. I've never met a normal one.

#HowToEatAsAHuman#

Going in Granddad's shed feels different these days. Ever since I've known that A LOT of people might be actually watching my vlog, I've felt a bit more pressure. Messages. Notifications. Lovely Gracie at school giving me a sentence-by-sentence critique of every vlog I do.

I still love doing it, though. This is the place where I can be most "me." It's like a massive dose of concentrated Millie Mountain Dew in the big glass of my life.

Note to me: I am not a soft drink. I am actually a spoon.

I sit on Granddad's old chair and tap RECORD.

> Hello! Millie here without Dave. She's currently eating my
> dinner. Which is sort of what I want to talk about. Hashtag
> Help show me how to share your lunch with your cat THE
> RIGHT WAY! Sometimes being a human is hard. I think cats
> actually have it really easy. Dave does. I make her breakfast
> for her. I get her gourmet tuna treats and never tell her that
> her breath stinks—even though it does. Badly. I style her
> fur every day. I check her for ticks. I don't have to do this

for any other living soul in my life. In fact I'm sure if I started checking my mum for ticks she'd be pretty furious.

Anyway, eating is harder than you think. I found this out today when I was so busy worrying about stuff that's going on in my life that I actually ignored my mouth. It's nice stuff, too. It's just new and I don't do new very well. Because of all this, my cat stole my hot dog. Dave actually twirled it around her head like a majorette. No, my mum didn't record it. That's because she's a mum.

But to make sure I can eat properly again I've been using a thing my mum does that helps my brain stop "catastrophizing." Or CAT-tastrophizing, where you think the worst AND Dave does some semi-evil feline thing.

Basically, I concentrate on the FACTS. As you can see, my granddad's shed is a bit . . . *(I try to find a nice way of saying it)* shabby chic. This is a fact. However, my catastrophizing worry brain says, "Granddad's shed is shabby chic." THEN it says, "OH MY GOD is this shed SO shabby that it's full of germs and is it also full of asbestos? And will that get in my lungs and am I breathing it in now and should these be fumigated by professionals TO SAVE MY LIFE?" . . . and any food I might try to eat just gets forgotten because my head is exploding.

When that happens, I just go back to the facts. Granddad's shed is a bit shabby chic and has a bird calendar in it that my cat likes to eat. And I STOP and I go do something else. And HONESTLY, that is it. I don't always manage it. That's why I lost my sausage—but I'm trying. And when it works, it just helps me through. And I can finish any meal without becoming a total spoon.

Anyway, thank you for watching. Leave any comments, and I'll see you next time.

And I put my thumb up at the end. I have no idea why I do this. As I upload it, Lauren messages me.

Mills. Need to CU. Come around. Plse

#Insects

Ever since Lauren and I had a fight, I've tried to put her first. I totally became a horrible friend and let my online life rule everything. I was a single-minded vlog robot. So now, when Lauren says she wants to see me, I go.

Her parents *really* don't get along. They throw shopping bags at each other on a regular basis. They aren't even living with each other at the moment, but they still have a war every time they meet. Lauren has told me she thinks she might be the result of a scientific experiment where they got two of the most unsuited human beings in history and forced them to have a child. I think this may be Lauren being a bit paranoid, but I can see her point. Her life does sound like a Marvel superhero's life. You know, overwhelming home life, and then one day you realize you can fly or that you're invisible. Well, she isn't that because we can all see her, but you know what I mean.

Lauren meets me at her front door. She's wearing her "I'm-so-excited-I-could-burst" face. She beckons me in, grabs both of my arms, and starts doing little jumps on the spot.

"I'm SO glad you're here!" she whispers. "I have just found out the most unbelievable thing! Are you ready for this?"

I don't think I am, but I don't think I've got any choice, either. I know my best friend. She looks like she might burst. Lauren takes a deep breath.

"Millie. Termites eat wood faster when they listen to rock music."

I start giggling. "C'mon, Lauren. That is just some bored pest controller man writing something random on Twitter for a joke and then someone believes it and . . ."

Lauren interrupts me. "No! I thought exactly the same thing, but I've read a ton of articles and I swear it's true. Clever people have confirmed it!"

I have an idea. "Okay. We should totally try to prove it. It could be a vlog! Hashtag Help the insects to eat my house faster! Well, you know what we need! We need termites."

Lauren looks at me. "There must be some in here. It's like a sanctuary for crawly things."

Lauren's house is honestly fine, but her dad and mum have spent so much time arguing over the years that the basic maintenance of the place has been ignored. This is extra strange as Lauren's dad is a KING Handyman!

The issue is you need teamwork to tile a bathroom, and you can't be a team when you're bringing up everything that the other one has ever done wrong EVER. Lauren says her mum makes a list of "bad memories" in the notes section of her phone so she can use them at will in arguments.

Lauren and I start to look for termites. We google what they look like, but we don't find any. Lauren reads that you can hear them eating your house if you put your ear up to a wall. She spends the next ten minutes with her face pressed up against every flat surface in the place. All we find is lots of dust (Gary would FREAK out!), a dead spider, and a slipper in the shape of a pizza that Lauren had when she was six. I post this on my Instagram page with #ShoeGoals.

#ShoeGoals

Lauren picks up my phone and pretends to vlog. "Hashtag
Help me prove that termites like tunes as they work! Sorry, guys! Sadly,
this amazingness could not be proven, as we couldn't find any willing
termites. In fact, we couldn't find any termites at all. Next time, join us
for Hashtag Help! Can giraffes swim? In fact, can they high-dive in an
emergency?"

This makes me really laugh. When Lauren goes on one of her fantasy trips, she's really funny. I don't know if anyone else would, but I
don't care. You know what best friends are like. You have tons of private
jokes between you that no one else gets.

I look at Lauren. "How are things here, anyway?"

Lauren looks down. "Oh, they're definitely splitting up, Mills. I'll be
staying here with Dad. Mum's gone to live with my aunt, but I see her
lots. It's better but, you know, I'm really down about it. I love both of
them, and they love me, but they just *hate* each other. Mum said she only
liked my dad for about twenty minutes in 2004. When they got married,
they had an argument about how to cut the wedding cake. Mum wanted
to do it with a normal knife. Dad wanted to do it on his own using a

ceremonial dagger someone had given him at a Latin American music festival in 1996. Yeah. It didn't look good from the start, really."

This is funny and sad at the same time.

I give Lauren a squeeze. My parents split up, but they still get along. I know this is a nightmare for her. I don't think she really got me around to see if insects like their music. I think she wanted a hug. I totally get that. If I were in her position, I'd want a hug 24/7.

"Let's go back to my house," I say. Lauren's coat is on before I finish the sentence.

#IReadTheComments

As soon as I open the front door at Mum's house, Dave attacks my ankle. This is the new normal.

Mum says animals don't understand fame, but if my cat had opposable thumbs she'd definitely be trying to offer you an autograph right now. I go to pet her these days and she either walks off with her tail poker-straight in the air and her butt wiggling OR she tries to bite me. I put up with all of it. She's one of the keys to being viral, and she knows it.

Mum is looking tense. I'm half expecting her to launch a full psychological investigation into the sausage incident, but she seems distracted and a bit angry. Gary is not here and, breaking news, his robot vacuum cleaner is not around, either. It still follows him around like a dog and he still calls it McWhirter. He's probably taken it out on the street for a dust and a walk.

Mum looks at both of us. She can sniff out that there's been some fun.

"What have you two been up to?" she asks. This makes us both giggle. "Oh, I don't want to know, actually. Gary's gone out. McWhirter's little wheels that help it roll around broke and it needs looking at."

I think I hear Mum mutter, "I think he needs looking at" under her breath, too.

"Anyway," she shouts, "I need to go get some milk. You two behave yourselves!"

Lauren falls into the big armchair and flops her legs over the sides. Gary would not approve of this, but Gary is not here. "Okay, Mills!" she exclaims. "Let's have a look at how your latest vlog is doing!"

I've been nervous about doing this because of what I told you before. The bigger it all gets, the more my brain becomes a mixture of excitement and total doom. I really want this to work. I want Mum to be proud. She's a go-getter. I don't want to be just a "slightly better." I'd never vlog that rhyme. It's dreadful.

My vlog has already got thousands of views and lots of likes. It's really weird thinking I'm in someone's "liked" file. Or in their history. Or—

Deep breaths. My ribs are beginning to hurt with all of this.

I focus my attention on the comments.

LOVE THIS. Love you Millie. Love your work. (People are lovely)

Shut up. No expert. Pull yourself together. Everything is a drama with you (Well, most people are lovely)

What's the thumb about? (Fair comment)

We need the cat. (This is harsh, but I get it)

Get Dave in. Dull without Dave (Bit too harsh)

Need more cat (Okay, I get the message)

Would be better with someone hot. (Oh, GO AWAY Sunshine Genius45738—you are clearly a nine-year-old boy)

Lauren leans over and reads. "Wow, Millie. Loads of views. You are getting bigger and bigger."

"Yeah," I mutter REALLY quickly. "Want to watch something on Netflix?"

Lauren knows what I'm doing. "Excellent change of subject. But you need to get used to this, Millie. This is your life now. You're sort of famous—"

At this precise moment Dave jumps on Lauren's shoulder.

"Sorry, Dave, yes!" Lauren says. "You are famous, too!"

Lauren is saying this as a joke, but I know that Dave totally understands what Lauren is saying and that she completely believes it. Dave falls into Lauren's lap and rubs against her chin for some attention. When Lauren isn't quick enough to give it to her, Dave punches her arm without using her claws. This is her latest party trick. Everyone thinks this aggression is cute—including Lauren.

"Oh, Davey-Lady," she says in a really silly voice, "are you being ignored by the horrible humans?"

Dave half closes her eyes in agreement. Lauren and I both start stroking her.

Lauren looks at me hard. "By the way, where's Danny going this weekend?"

I sigh. "Oh, he's going with his parents to some kind of spa. Facials. Pedicures. That sort of thing. He can't really text me much because they are in the middle of nowhere. So it will probably be all massage. No message."

I'm quite proud of this joke, but Lauren completely ignores it.

Lauren looks down at Dave. "Must be weird wanting to spend time with your parents. I couldn't relax with mine—even if I'd had an anesthetic. I don't even mean local anesthetic. It would have to be general. I'd need complete unconsciousness."

Lauren is really getting good at the dark humor thing. I don't know whether I should laugh or just hug her again. Instead, I say what's been on my mind for a few days.

"To be honest, Loz, Danny doesn't generally message me as often as I thought he might do. Even when he's not in the middle of a forest having microdermabrasion he's not really . . . very . . ."

"Into you?" Lauren blurts out. I know she doesn't mean to be so blunt, but this STINGS.

"No. He likes me. I think he's into me. We've spent quality time together. It's going really good, but . . ."

How do I explain this to Lauren? You know when you've got a tiny bit of peanut butter left in the jar and you have to spread it really thinly over your toast to make it work? Danny is that peanut butter. He is spread very thinly. His parents love him. His friends love him. I love him. So we all get little bursts of his buttery time. And like I've said before, he's so relaxed sometimes he's practically asleep. He's Zen. In fact, he's his own brand of Zen. He's Danny Zen—*Zan*. I LOVE that about him, but sometimes I want him to be more a part of my life and more a part of my vlog.

He puts his phone away too much. I try to be cool with it, but he puts it down in his room and doesn't check it for hours. I'm not like that. I'm a bit more . . . look, I love my friends and I love my phone. I just wish Danny were a bit more . . . present? OH NO. I SOUND PATHETIC.

"Oh, Lauren," I say with a tut. "I think love might have turned my wise-woman button off and my obsessive-girlfriend button on."

"Not you, Mills," Lauren scoffs. "You'll be sensible till you die. That's what Hashtag Help is all about. Solid advice! OUCH!"

Dave scratches Lauren with her claws extended.

"And you, Dave, obviously," Lauren snaps.

That was absolutely not a coincidence. I'm sure Dave can understand just about everything that we are saying. Knowing Dave, she can probably speak several languages. She already knows English and Cat. She'll be learning coding next and, after that, it'll be Dave World Domination.

#SchoolLegend

When I wake up on Monday morning, the first thing I'm *STILL* thinking about is SunshineGenius45738 and the "Would be better with someone hot" comment.

Of course this is what I am thinking about. If there are 100 people saying nice things and one total troll saying sexist nonsense GUESS WHO HAS WALKED TO THE FRONT OF MY BRAIN WHILST I'VE BEEN ASLEEP?! SunshineGenius45738 presses the button in me that thinks all this is just a crazy burst of luck and I'm going to be found out as just someone with quite a good cat. GO AWAY, BRAIN BURP OF INFERIORITY.

This is my new reality. Telling people I don't know to remove themselves from my head as their comments are irrelevant and haters gonna hate.

That's not the only thing that has changed.

Walking into school these days involves some points and whispers. You know the sort of thing. People putting their hands up to hide their mouths when they see you (obvious!) OR people turning their back, giggling and then pointing (even more obvious and rude!). I'm not being paranoid. You can ask Lauren. I have to make sure I do schoolwork really well as teachers have made snarky comments like, "YOU can't make a career out of being on the Internet talking about random things!" Actually, you can, and I'd like to for the moment—and there is nothing wrong with that.

It's amazing how people think you're getting arrogant when inside you're feeling just relieved and excited and satisfied and nervous and you're going around like a washing machine on a HOT MESS SPIN CYCLE.

Lauren thinks teachers wouldn't even say that if I were a boy. If it were a boy doing a #Help vlog, they'd be congratulating him on doing such a positive thing and saying things like, "Isn't it wonderful to see a sensitive man trying to help people like that?!" Plus, they'd all be asking him for his autograph for their children and taking him to important meetings in London and stopping at Starbucks on the way. "Yes, of course you can have a caramel latte with an extra shot and a danish. I'll pay, Corey. It's fine!"

Corey doesn't exist and this IS probably a bit farfetched, but if a boy does anything in this school that doesn't involve fighting, bullying, skipping school, or destroying stuff, teachers go overboard. A girl does something good and they just pull the biggest MEH meme face in history.

You can tell my imagination is running pretty wild. I need twenty minutes of mindfulness. Or twenty years.

Luckily, I don't have much time to concentrate on my whirlwind brain as I see my boyfriend hurtling toward me like the world's most lush missile. His hair is incredible. He looks like a walking statue. I'm sure he has a stylist waiting by his front door every day. It's probably his mum with a really good detangling hairbrush, but STILL he looks as sleek as an incredibly healthy and handsome dolphin. The cleverest dolphin. He doesn't just jump through hoops for fish. He does quantum physics, too, with his fin. His spa retreat really did him good.

Danny stretches his arms around me. He smells like a mixture of laundry powder and mints. It doesn't sound that nice, but if it were an aftershave they would call it L'Eau de Beautiful Homme.

I'm trying to be a bit less of a gushy girlfriend and a bit more of a feminist powerhouse, so I don't give him a full squeeze, just a casual back-tightening.

"Hello, Lady Millie," he purrs.

"Hello, you," I say breezily. Mum says to treat ALL men like you'd treat the mailman—friendly but with a distance.

I tackle him directly. "You didn't text me!"

Danny looks down, shuffles his feet from side to side, and then kicks some imaginary dirt. It must be imaginary. We are standing on concrete and we have the bossiest, cleanest school custodian in the history of mankind.

"Yeah, I'm just trying to be more . . . in the moment," Danny says. "When we weren't doing spa stuff I was watching lots of programs about the ocean. We all need to use less plastic, you know, Millie. The sea is this amazing place. There's a lake at the bottom of the ocean. A saltwater lake! Also, and I don't know how to break this to you, some sea turtles breathe through their butts."

This makes me really smile. In fact, I really want to guffaw like a maniac, but I don't want to be a tedious "giggle at everything boys say" sort of girl, so I just think of something terrible. That's a top tip of mine. If you need to stop laughing at something (this is particularly handy in school), think of your cat running away or breaking your nose in a freak lamppost accident.

Danny smiles. "This is serious, Millie! We must protect the endangered rears of marine animals!" But he laughs, too. "Anyway, Mills. Better go to class. See you later!"

He pecks me on the cheek and runs off. I stand there thinking why on earth don't I just TELL HIM HOW MUCH I MISS HIM when he's not around?! Why don't I tell him I want to see him more and I want him to just message me even if it's once a day. I don't want to be pathetic, but I want to be in a relationship that feels a bit more . . . real.

At that moment my phone beeps. It's Lauren.

> Where R U? U R not sick R U? PLEASE DON'T BE! I can't face history without you. PS HAVE U SEEN YOU KNOW WHO?!

Lauren has this sixth sense that only best friends have. I'm feeling uncomfortable, and magically she texts. I'm feeling sad, and she messages me a cat video. I'm feeling worried and—

Oh no.

Erin Breeler is standing straight in front of me.

#BrandNewErin

Erin Breeler used to be the social media QUEEN. At school we lived and died by her every post. As soon as you got the notification of ANYTHING she did—you looked. It was like the law.

Erin used to make my life a living hell.

Things have changed. Not so long ago, Erin standing in front of me would have been the worst start to a school week since I was eight and accidentally spent an entire Monday with a huge cornflake in my hair. No one needs cereal dandruff. That was bad, but I would have preferred that to Old Erin. Old Erin was MEAN.

New Erin is different. New Erin is still gorgeous as ever, but she's actually managed to turn into a human with feelings that you can relate to. Also, she seems a bit . . . lonely. In fact, she's kind of sad. Ever since she was outed as Mr. Style Shame, her world has changed a lot. Mr. Style Shame was the Instagram account that humiliated everyone within a 100-mile radius of the school. It caught you at your very worst moment and posted it for entertainment (including poor Lauren's high-heel disaster). Erin was behind it, and once we all found out, she deleted it. All of Erin's social media accounts have lost loads of followers, and because of that, shops and designers don't send her anything. She's not an influencer anymore. She's just one of us now, completely harmless. The Goddess is gone.

I feel bad for her. I know I probably shouldn't because she made my life a living misery, but lately she's seemed so defeated.

None of this explains why I am feeling sick and why my heart is pounding out of my chest. Mum would call this "muscle memory." Your body reacts to a previous threat whether you want it to or not, EVEN when that threat has disappeared. Erin is the tarantula who bit me, but who has now lost her fangs of doom. I'm still terrified of her, though.

Erin with eight perfectly tanned, toned legs—that's a terrible thought.

"Hello, Millie," Erin says very softly. She doesn't so much stand as float. She's a wasp in a really nice coat. No, not a wasp—a bee. She probably could still sting, but she can be cute, too.

"How are you?" I manage to get out. In my head she's still loaded with potential danger.

"Oh, you know," she groans, "I'm just trying to be a better me."

If this were a daytime talk show, we'd all be clapping for her now. But it's not. It's my school.

Erin keeps talking. "No one really talks to me these days. It's just . . . I'm trying to be different. I know I did wrong. I'm trying to be a better me. Does that make sense?"

It does. I totally get what she is saying. We've all done things we regret. We've all done wrong. Erin did REALLY bad stuff, but she knows about her fashion. She knows about style. She totally gets going viral and she understands the world I'm now in. Perhaps she could . . .

A thought flashes through my head like a greyhound that's seen a really big bone. I let it go, though, as it would cause trouble. BIG trouble.

Instead, I try some comforting stuff. "You could always start again, you know. All your skills are getting wasted. Perhaps you could do something else online, but just something that isn't . . . evil."

Erin gives me a hurt, hard stare.

"I don't mean evil!" I blurt. I think I save myself. "I mean, something positive that lifts people up! You can make people look incredible! Why not start again with something totally new?"

Erin sighs. "Perhaps," she murmurs. "Anyway, it's going great for you. You're doing so—"

I interrupt her immediately. I can't cope with sudden vocal compliment outbursts yet. "Yeah!" I say. "Not too bad. Anyway, we better get going. See you soon!"

#MyMouth

Lauren is looking at me like I'm completely insane. We are just waiting for class to begin.

"Why did you say that to her?!"

"I don't know!" I snap. "I was trying to . . . I don't even know what I was trying to do. I just felt sorry for her. She's had a hard time!"

"Completely of her own making!" Lauren shouts. "She wrecked lives! She posted photos of me that are still being shared everywhere. There's a gang of ninth-grade boys who still call me Cinderella because I left my shoe behind! Now you're encouraging her to start again! In what universe does she deserve a second chance?!"

There's a big pause.

"Some burglars only get six months!" I say.

I am running out of arguments.

"Okay then, Lauren." I'm getting angry now. "How long should we punish trolls for?"

She thinks for about two seconds. "For an eternity," she snaps. "Erin Breeler should not be part of our lives. She doesn't deserve a second chance. Though"—Lauren softens a bit—"she is apparently responsible for something fairly incredible and amazing. . . ."

#Brad

"That," Lauren proudly exclaims, "that is...what I was messaging you about! That is what everyone is talking about."

Bradley Sanderson, who previously was the greatest geek on the planet, has changed.

Bradley's hair has been restyled into something that makes him look like he's from one of those old films you see on vintage stations when you're flicking through the channels. A brooding hero. A star. Do I sound like a twonk? Yes. But I am also speaking the truth. He looks taller, and he's walking differently with his head up and a semi-smile. His dorky glasses are the same, but they seem uber-cool dripping off his nose now. This is Bradley 2.0, and it is wonderful.

It's also confusing.

Bradley and I are sort of unfinished business. He helped me a lot with #Help. He understands it because he runs a very successful vlog called The King of Elevation, which is entirely about elevators and escalators. Yes, I know that sounds very dull, but Bradley makes it interesting. Once you understand the workings of a Schindler 5500 and its optimum space configurability (ask Bradley what that means), you can look at going up and down in a whole new way.

I had an odd, stirry tummy, and warm feelings for Bradley. Then we kissed, but we shouldn't have. I liked Danny, Danny and me happened, I put Bradley in the friend zone, and Bradley got hurt. He asked me to give him space and he has used that space to make himself really hot.

Boys are confusing.

Lauren stares at me and purses her lips. "That, Millie, is a classic revenge makeover. You reject him. He, like an ignored rosebush in the garden, waters himself and blooms."

Lauren has gone full spoon. This makes me giggle.

"Seriously, Millie." Lauren is getting annoyed. "That's what he's done. And do you know who is apparently responsible for that? Erin."

You can say what you like about Erin (and we all have), but what she's done to Bradley is incredible. It proves she's changed, too. Erin was always horrible to Bradley. She didn't like boys like him. He wasn't in her "tribe." But perhaps he is now. Bradley is lovely underneath it all. He would give anyone a second chance.

"Erin has made him into an Adidas," Lauren says proudly.

"I think you mean Adonis, Loz," I reply.

"Whatever," Lauren says. "The fact is, he's red-hot geek hot."

We have to stop talking because for the first time in what seems a very long time, Bradley is looking at me. He smiles, waves, and gets up to talk to us.

"Oh, HELLO," Lauren whispers to me. "Looks like someone wants to be friends again."

#JustTheWayYouAre

Bradley slumps beside us. His navy wool coat is far too big for him, but it looks really good. He smells a bit musty, but it's a good musty. It's the smell of old books and antiques that you shove in your wardrobe for years and turn out to be worth a fortune.

"Hello, Bradley!" Lauren is loving this, I can tell. "This is a whole new look, isn't it?"

"Yeah," he says really casually. "I just felt like shaking things up a bit, you know."

"And Erin helped you?" Lauren asks. I jab her with my elbow. She knows this is a naughty thing to say. Her eyes go wide and she wiggles her fingers.

Bradley looks down and plays with his pockets. "Yeah. I felt a bit sorry for her. And she's talented with looks stuff. That's not my thing, but as I always say, get the experts involved. She knows jumpers and coats. I know machines."

"And have you helped her up any escalators recently, Bradley?" Lauren asks. She's trying to act innocent but we all know what she means.

I knock Lauren so hard that I think Bradley notices. He also knows EXACTLY what Lauren is implying.

"No. It's just professional. I'm single and happy," Bradley announces proudly. "It is possible, Lauren, for males and females to just be colleagues."

Lauren looks at me with a bit of shame. I believe him. Bradley doesn't lie. But the thought of Bradley spending even non-loved-up time with another woman makes me feel odd. It's the same feeling I get when I see Danny chatting to another girl for too long. It feels like ants on bicycles are riding through your stomach—you're very angry that they are using your tummy as a velodrome and you want to just push them all over and puncture their wheels.

I think this feeling might be jealousy.

At this moment, Lauren decides that she needs to go and talk to someone. She doesn't say who. This leaves me and Bradley. Just sitting there. In silence.

This is not good. Silence feels prickly. I get up to go to class and Bradley tugs gently at my bag.

"Come on then, Millie Porter. Hashtag Help me. Tell me what's been going on with you?"

I sit back down.

#StayYOU

I don't know how to handle this. I think this is probably Bradley's way of saying, "Let's be friends again," but it feels really strange. I still feel bad about how I treated him. I decide to be factual again. It's always a sound plan. Stick to the facts.

"Good!"

This is my completely useless Millie one-word answer.

Bradley smiles at me. "I know it's been going well for you. I've watched all your stuff. You're great. You come across really well."

He knows I struggle with the whole confidence thing. This is a really sweet thing to say.

"I don't *feel* great at it, Bradley," I confess. "I want this to work. I want it to be big. But to be honest, I'm finding it hard. I can't quite believe what has happened. I keep expecting something to go horribly wrong and everyone is going to discover—"

Bradley interrupts. "Stop thinking that way! You are rocking this. What you've got, Millie, is a classic case of impostor syndrome. It's when you doubt yourself constantly. You need to stop it. You're very good at what you do."

41

I look at him. He has pushed his glasses down so I can see into his eyes.

"Thank you," I manage to blurt. It's good to have Bradley back in my life.

Then I do something silly. For whatever reason, my jaw again detaches itself from my brain and decides to ask Bradley, "Are you single? Come on, you can tell me."

As the words fall out of my mouth, I know it's the wrong thing to say.

Bradley goes a bit frosty and mumbles, "No. I told you before. Even if I was, it is no one's business. It's certainly not your business."

This feels harsh. I think Bradley realizes he's gone too far, because he changes the subject fast.

"What's next for you then, Millster?"

I look through my bag and pretend to reorganize it. When my hands are doing something, I can say things I'm struggling with in a better way. Classic nervous fidgeting. I pull out my pencil case, some tea tree oil, and a squeaky mouse. A squeaky mouse?

Dave!

Dave has a habit of dumping things in my belongings. I should probably be grateful it's not an actual dead mouse.

"What's next for me is I've got a meeting after school tomorrow with someone who manages vloggers. Lydia Portancia. She calls herself a 'life content creator.' She thinks she can help me take Hashtag Help to a new level. I want to grow what I've already got, but . . ."

Suddenly, Bradley takes hold of my right hand. It's the one with the toy mouse in it. It squeaks. This is funny, but Bradley is deadly serious.

"Don't lose yourself, Millie. You're fine as you are. Don't let anyone change your thing. Listen to what they have got to say, but you don't *have* to follow their plans. You are fine as you are." He squeaks the mouse again. "And Dave is fine, too. Give her a pet from me. See you around."

With that, Bradley gorgeously geeks away.

"Don't lose yourself, Millie."

"You are just fine."

This is very sensible advice.

What is not sensible is standing on your own like a spoon holding your cat's raggedy toy in the drizzly rain. It's not a good look. I go to class and squeak Dave's mouse all the way there.

#Meeting

I didn't sleep last night. School's over, but I feel like a total zombie. Getting up at 5:00 a.m. after falling asleep at 4:43 a.m. is NOT a good idea. Eight minutes' sleep does not give you a clear head.

Eight minutes' sleep also means you can't even do basic math.

I got through the day, but I didn't learn anything. Information sploshed off me and nothing soaked in. It felt like I was walking round with a mini tornado on my head that turned just in the middle of my eyes. It's difficult to think about osmosis and the Civil War when there's a major weather condition doing its thing on your face.

Mum and I are in the car on the way to meet the agent and she keeps asking me if I'm okay. I tell her I am, but I am not. The truth is I'm very, very worried about meeting the agent. I can tell this for the following reasons:

1. In addition to the tornado, a hurricane, a cyclone, and a drought are now happening all over my forehead and chin. My cheeks are also on fire. Blotchy red is not a good look. The government has declared my face a disaster zone and the army is currently evacuating the area.

2. My body is in a knot. I had a necklace once that had a knot in it that was impossible to undo. I threw it out of my bedroom window in a temper. My body definitely feels like cheap jewelry you should defenestrate.

3. *Defenestrate* is the best word ever. Granddad threatens everyone with it. It means to throw something out of a window.

4. My granddad would never really defenestrate anyone, by the way. His hips and knees are too weak. He'd need the help of a winch.

5. I am worried about the earth leaving its orbit and heading nearer or farther away from the sun. Which would I choose? Boil or freeze to death? Probably freeze.

6. Forget freezing to death. No one looks good in a heavily quilted jacket.

7. I've eaten two bars of chocolate and a brie and red onion relish baguette. It's pure stress hunger. I HATE red onion relish. Why do they always let brie suffer? Brie is the queen of cheese. She should be able to sit on her throne alone without stinky bits of root vegetables.

It hits me.

I'm just about to meet someone and have catastrophically bad onion breath. The sort of breath that stops traffic and the police are called and they put DO NOT CROSS tape across your face. Nice one, Millie. I check it with Mum. She grimaces, turns her head to the side, and gives me a squirt of breath freshener. I close my eyes and try to focus. A bit of mindfulness. Think about the nice things in life—music, coconut ice cream, the smile of a Danny, Dave when she spots a can of tuna and tries to open the can with her paws and then, when that fails, her tongue.

All this is interrupted by seven of the most frightening words in the history of mankind.

"Can we have a chat now, Millie?"

Here's a warning: Parents are slightly evil. I mean, they can be snake-like with their cunning. Mum has hidden behind the wheel in a tight coil and is now bursting out with fangs to interrogate me. I'm cornered. I can't get off. We are in something that is going 80 mph and has child-proof locked doors. Mum even controls the volume to the radio. I've witnessed some songs by a group called the Backstreet Boys that no one should have to hear. This car can be like a prison cell. A prison cell with really bad tunes about everybody rocking their body in the correct way.

Mum takes a big breath. "I know you're getting your head around everything that is going on. I saw your last vlog. Whatever happens in this meeting, just see all this as . . . froth on your coffee."

Froth on my coffee. I'm about to have one of the most important meetings ever and Mum is saying it's like the top of a hot drink. Mum has explained to me that she has a brain like mine! She, of ALL people, should understand that keeping calm when the stakes are THIS high is IMPOSSIBLE. I can feel my face collapsing. I do not have a poker face, as Aunty Teresa calls it. I wear my emotions like a very loud shirt.

Mum can see I look confused and tries to explain.

"I mean, this is just a wonderful experience. It's not the REALLY important stuff of life. It's just fun. FUN! F. U. N. Something to enjoy and have a laugh with Lauren about!"

I've noticed that when someone says something is going to be fun, it's not. If it really is going to be fun, you don't need to label it.

This is when I have to tell Mum I feel a lot differently about it. All this is very important to me because I want everything I do to go viral. I like to get things RIGHT and a lot of people see my posts. Probably everyone. And they'll all have an opinion on it and feedback and comments and trolls. Basically, trolls doing their trolling thing.

Mum stares at me. "Work out who matters and concentrate on the facts. Something else, too, Millie. Don't sweat the small stuff."

Mum says this with a wink.

Don't sweat the small stuff. That phrase was never designed for me. I sweat all sizes of stuff. I do not discriminate. If it's big, I worry, and if it's tiny, I worry. Mum says I run an equal-opportunity kind of anxiety. She's right.

#LydiaPortancia

When we finally do arrive at Lydia Portancia's office, we are late. Very late. We are also flustered, with red faces and frizzy hair. This is because we got really lost. Mum asked everyone for directions, from a street cleaner to a tourist from Beijing who has only been in the city for three days. She showed us where we should go. We might as well be wearing signs that say, WE DO NOT HAVE A CLUE WHAT WE ARE DOING AND WE NEED HELP FROM EVERYONE.

For the record, this includes people who are on a trip of a lifetime and really could do without having to help two lost people. Mum told her she should go to the Victoria and Albert Museum. The tourist told Mum she had been twice already and had sketched the entire Elizabethan fashion section.

I also do not think our appearance is the right "look" for a business meeting. I mean, I've never had a business meeting before, but in my gut, this feels wrong and my gut has a brain of its own that is *very* often right. Also, it's very unlike Mum. She's always so prepared for things like this. Perhaps she has a lot on her mind. She seems a bit distracted.

I know the feeling.

The receptionist greets us and we have to sign in and wear name tags. Mum has a special place on her jacket for hers. I try to copy her, but it feels a bit like I'm wearing a LOOK AT ME!! MY NAME IS MILLIE!! brooch. It's conspicuous—it might as well have flashing lights on it. I usually like being anonymous. I know that sounds faintly ridiculous as I now vlog to . . . let's just call it "a lot" of people. Don't ask me to do actual numbers, as they make me feel a bit sick. Mum calls them "stadium" numbers. Stadiums. People piled high on top of each other in seats all looking at me. I imagine all my subscribers being at a football game and everyone pulling a "What the hell?!" face as I sing the national anthem and get the second line wrong.

Just as I'm becoming a national disgrace in my head, Mum distracts me by pointing at a poster that says KEEP CALM AND VLOG.

I don't know what it is about "Keep Calm" posters, but they always have the opposite effect on me. They just make me all sweaty. They basically tell you there is something to be worried about. It's like someone yelling "KEEP CALM!" at you whilst your house is on fire and your cat is still stuck inside.

Of course, knowing Dave, she'd be walking through the fire dragging humans out and still looking feline-glam like some kind of FUR-QUEEN.

From the corner of my eye, I see a firework go off. It's Lydia Portancia. She's very flamboyant. Nails with clouds on them. Flouncy patterned scarves.

"Millie, what a joy! I feel like I know you!" she screams. "You have this incredible ability to bring warmth to the screen. Vulnerability, yet— I think you'd call it—sass!"

She does this double kiss thing. I manage to kiss one cheek and then kiss the random air. This is standard.

Lydia looks to either side of my arms and grins. "Where's Dave?"

Did she seriously expect me to bring the cat?

"Er . . . she's not the best traveler," I mutter. "She attaches herself to the ceiling of the cat cage when we take her to the vet. She defies gravity very easily!"

Lydia does a too-big laugh. I mean, what I said was kind of funny, but it wasn't hilarious.

Finally, Lydia gets around to Mum.

"And you're Millie's mum! Hello! Delighted to meet you!"

Lydia does not embrace my mother. This is because my mum is standing in a position that makes a hug impossible. She thrusts her arm out like a missile and does her trademark boa constrictor business handshake.

"Yes, I'm Millie's mum. Please call me Ms. Porter, though. I'm very proud of my daughter, but I think it's very important for us all to be framed within our nonmaternal roles as women. Millie has my name. I don't believe in possessive, patriarchy-driven titles."

I know my mum. This is her no-messing "A" game. It's "bring it on!" feminism, and it's magnificently scary. If I were Lydia, I'd feel slightly weirded out and probably slightly frightened.

Lydia, though, seems totally unfazed. She throws her hands in the air and says, "My dear, I TOTALLY understand! My husband's name was Smith. There was no way on earth I was taking THAT on and losing my Renaissance roots! Now"—she turns to a young girl scurrying behind her—"rooibos tea, please, Samantha. Touch of honey and an Oreo. Now, drinks! Coffee? Yes? YES!" She doesn't give us time to answer, but Mum answers anyway. "Actually, can I have tea, please? Milk, no sugar. And Millie will have the same. We are not big coffee drinkers. We don't need artificial energy."

This is not in any sense fully true, but I am not prepared to argue with Mum in any way, shape, or form right now.

Lydia sits down in her chair. I say chair, but it's more like a throne. It has plump purple cushions and ornate gold framework. She holds each arm and sits up poker-straight. It's definitely regal. Our chairs are a lot lower than hers and a lot less fancy.

Mum gets in first. "So, tell me, Lydia," she pronounces, "what is the strategy for my daughter?"

Lydia takes a deep breath. "Well, the strategy is to link Millie to other vloggers and influencers. It's about gently promoting her product. Branded merchandise will get sent to her for free for her to mention and then, depending on her growth of course, people will pay her to promote their products. It will probably start with pet food companies and pet accessories."

I find my mouth yelling out, "Dave won't touch anything with lamb!"

I realize that sounds a bit dramatic, so I elaborate. "I mean, she used to love it, but she hates it now. She has phases. She had a massive turkey thing going on, and then she dropped her blue-ringed octopus in a turkey and vegetable gourmet broth and . . ."

Lydia interrupts, "Aren't blue-ringed octopuses deadly?"

I realize I sound completely insane. Why isn't Mum flying in to save me from my own brain?!

I try to explain. "Oh, the blue-ringed octopus is just a toy. It's Dave's favorite thing. My friend's dad brought it back from Sydney. It's not poisonous. Well, it probably would be if you ate it all, but Dave just dribbles on it, mainly. The point is, I can't make Dave eat stuff she doesn't want to eat!"

There is a long pause whilst everyone, including me, tries to work out what I just said.

Lydia clearly decides that she is going to ignore my mind blurt and carry on with her very logical train of thought.

"I've looked at the last vlog. Millie, it's wonderful. If I can just add a teensy caveat?"

I don't know what one of these is, but I'll google it later.

Lydia stares at me hard. "Just more cat. Dave is a key part of your brand. We need maximum Dave at all points! Any opportunity to get her in the vlog, however tenuous, is a FANTASTIC opportunity! We need maximum Dave at all points!"

I can tell immediately that Lydia is a dog person. Dog people expect things to do as they are told. Dog people expect things to sit and do tricks. Cat people like me know through Dave that life is fundamentally ALL chaos and that you can't control anything.

I try to explain this politely, but it comes out a bit exasperated. "She's a cat. She's quite hard to control."

At times like this, I wish I could go to my Zen Loo and just get my thoughts together.

Lydia seems to have her answer already prepared.

"Incentivize her! It's simple. I appreciate that she's a fussy eater. Most divas are! Try treats. Expensive treats. NEVER be afraid to go salmon. Atlantic, not tinned. Lightly steamed! Add a little mayonnaise to it. Make her feel special. I tend to find if you make these creatures feel important, they respond with a better performance—whether they are human or feline!"

Mum makes an "I beg your pardon?!" face. We don't get to eat that sort of food on a regular basis. Also, it involves a certain degree of cook-

52

ing skill. I can't see Gary the Neat Freak cooking individual meals for Dave. He barely tolerates her as it is.

What we have learned from this whole exchange is that Lydia is definitely very rich and that she has a poodle—a professionally trained one, at that. It was probably from a circus, is perfectly groomed at all times, and is totally obedient. This is the opposite of Dave. I mean, she keeps herself neat but she is also chill enough these days to have half a hedge attached around her body and not really give two hoots. She certainly never does what anyone asks her to.

I can see all this is leading to one thing that I don't feel I can talk about at all.

"So, money," Mum declares. She gets straight to it. This is a woman who does massive deals every week. Zero prisoners are taken. Mum says to go straight for the jugular. Close the deal. It's an art, she has always told me—the art of the deal! She used to say this a lot until she realized it was also the title of a book by Donald Trump. Now she says it hardly ever.

Mum continues. She sounds so TOUGH.

"What sort of money are you going to take from my daughter for your representation?"

Lydia is completely unperturbed. "I won't take anything till Millie actually starts earning money. Then we can think about full contracts and things like that. We'll obviously be looking for verification from all the platforms that she is on."

"Verification of what?" Mum asks. She's confused. How many times have I explained this?! It's still not going into her head.

Lydia smiles. I think she quite likes the fact that Mum doesn't understand something.

"Verification. Usually a little symbol that just confirms that you're 'you,' as it were. It can be something like a blue checkmark. Immediately, your potential in every way increases. It just gives you more credibility. More social media power!"

Mum looks really unimpressed, but keeps it professional. "And how do we get that?"

Lydia pops her head onto her shoulder and takes a big sigh.

"Well, it depends completely on the platform Millie is appearing on. I'm not sure of the complete criteria. If I'm honest, I don't think anyone fully is."

This response does not make Mum happy. She goes full-on sarcastic.

"So, a totally random person decides whether my daughter has a check next to her name to make her 'credible.' It's a brave new world!"

Mum says this in such a way that I *know* she is thinking it's a BAD new world and not a brave one.

I want my mum to look after the business parts for me, but I don't want her to mess this up for me either.

Lydia tries to reassure Mum. "I understand it sounds a bit odd, but Ms. Porter, this is all very new territory. Certainly, for women of our generation who were probably lucky to have one phone line in the house! I'd really encourage you to spend some time online yourself. I don't mean just on Netflix. I mean having a look at other social influencers, other vloggers, and check out how they conduct themselves and look at just what successful brands they've become."

Mum nods. "Lydia," she pronounces, "this has certainly given us a lot to think about. I think we are both prepared to enter into this preliminary arrangement with you. Obviously, we'll have to see how it goes, and I will be monitoring the situation very closely."

This statement has two effects. First, I feel about six years old and vaguely furious. Second, Lydia is absolutely delighted.

"This is wonderful news!" she shouts, and leaps out of her throne to give me another air-kissy semi-hug weird thing. She shakes Mum's hand very firmly. It's almost like they are wrestling.

"That's a deal, then!" Lydia sort of yells.

"Yes," Mum says, "it's a kind of deal until we get something more firm in place. Something more formal."

My mum always has to have the final word.

In the car on the way back, I'm quiet. This is because I am annoyed. My mum's brain drill can feel this.

"Millie," she says, again when we are hurtling along at high speed in a car I can't escape from, "I know you probably felt a bit patronized in there, and I can understand that. But the thing is, you are still very young, with not a lot of business experience. I have lots, and I'm not going to apologize for it. I know how to talk to people without giving an inch. You're the most important person in my life. You always will be. That's why I took over. You've shown you can do your thing brilliantly online. Let me do my thing brilliantly offline."

Mum is fantastic at this. She gives you a huge compliment so you can't really argue with anything else she has said. I'm still angry, though, so I have to say something.

"I just felt a bit left out, that's all. You did the full feminist name-intro classic, then you totally took over ALL the financial stuff. All the 'Let's talk money,' and then YOU closed the deal. I wanted to shut the deal door. Or whatever you call it."

"I get it," Mum sort of whispers, "but trust me, Millie, it was for the best."

"It was for the best." Let's hope so. At the moment, it just feels like in the most important meeting of my life, I was a huge spare part. An extra. One of those people who get a tiny amount of money every day to sit behind someone more important in a TV show and pretend to talk. According to Lauren, they just say the word *rhubarb* repeatedly.

I am the rhubarb girl. Mum is the major star. No, Dave is. Dave is the Lady Gaga of our house. The meeting was mainly about her and she didn't even go. She WOULDN'T even go.

I feel like all this has gone wrong.

#HowDidItGo?

By the time we get home it's quite late, but Mum lets Danny in to talk for a few minutes. This is probably because she feels a bit guilty for treating me like a toddler when I am the actual brand. I sound a bit like a diva, but I don't like being talked over. She may be my manager, but I can guarantee that Ariana Grande's mum does NOT treat her like that. They are a real TEAM effort.

Danny is excited. "How did it go?!" he screams.

I just groan, "Rhubarb, rhubarb, rhubarb," and then realize Danny doesn't have psychic abilities.

"It went okay." I sigh. "The thing is, she wants cats."

Danny starts giggling. "Perhaps you can get a cat cam. Have you seen *Animals with Cameras*? They put a camera around cheetahs' necks!! You get to see everything. Sleep. Eating. Killing stupid gazelles by running at sixty miles an hour and grabbing them by the neck."

That's the wildlife version of what Mum was trying to do to Lydia Portancia today in the meeting.

I stare at Danny. I'm not really in the mood for silly. I'm a bit of a grump.

"One, that would cost a fortune. Two, I don't want to cramp Dave's style. Can you imagine what it's like to go out and meet the other cats in the neighborhood? 'What's that around your neck, Dave? Honestly, buddy, it looks a bit ridiculous.' I'm all for statement accessories, but that's too much."

This makes Danny laugh a lot. It's very cool being a woman who makes handsome men collapse with the giggles. Mum says it's a superpower.

"I can't stay around for long," Danny says once he's finished wiping his eyes. "Big day tomorrow. Dad has called a BIG family meeting."

I stare at him and then squint. "That sounds a bit ominous."

Danny doesn't look too fussed. "Millie, in my experience it could be about anything from 'Shall we get a gerbil?' to 'What's for dinner on Sunday?' to 'Your grandma has decided she wants to do a sky-dive at age eighty-six and I think we should absolutely talk her out of it considering her arthritis.' It could be ANYTHING. I take life as it comes."

Zen Dan. Zan. He always takes life as it hurtles his way.

"Anyway," Danny says, "got to go. Millie, can I say something a bit uncomfortable? I think you should enjoy yourself a bit more. Stop focusing on all the bad stuff in your life. Start thinking about the good stuff. You have an incredible family and great friends. Don't make it ALL about the vlog. I'm not saying don't do it. Just lighten up a bit."

I wish I could just lighten up, but I am not naturally Zan like Danny. I take life in a panic. Mostly it's controlled, but sometimes it's plummeting to earth and I've forgotten to open my parachute.

But then we kiss and my parachute DOES open and I land on the ground in a heap but crucially not dead. No, you should NOT rely on boys to make you feel better (I CAN HEAR YOU IN MY HEAD, MUM!), but occasionally they do help. They are a nice distraction from a head of doom.

After Danny leaves, I check my phone.

There are three notifications. There's a text from Lauren, **How did it go KWEEEENNN?!**, a WhatsApp from Bradley, **Hope you got a good deal** (this is SO Bradley—zero messing about), and a message from Granddad. You can tell Aunty Teresa has helped him to write it, as it makes actual sense.

Hello, Millie! What country does this flag belong to?! Don't cheat! Come around tomorrow after school and tell me. Have your tea here, too, and that's an order!

It's a lovely flag. It's got people on it, but I have no idea. One of them is holding an axe but not in a way that makes him look like he's in a horror film and he's going to do something appalling. He just looks like he's holding it because he's going to chop down a tree and build a tremendous beach house. Don't ask me how, I can just tell.

I've never seen this flag before in my life. I could do a Google image reverse search but Granddad can always tell when I'm lying. He says my ears do this mad involuntary wiggle thing.

I just hope Teresa hasn't done what she's been threatening to do for years—turn Granddad's house into a microstate so she doesn't have to pay any tax. Creating her own flag is exactly the sort of thing that she would do. And the men on it are bare chested. It's basically an Aunty Teresa fantasy with a bit of graphic design from an app. I bet she declares herself queen, president for life, gets hippos as pets, and goes completely wild.

I've decided I'm giving up on trivia. It stresses me out completely.

#Desert-ion

The next day, Granddad is waiting to pounce on me as soon as I get into his house. "Come on then, Millie!" he shouts. "What was the flag?!"

I have a couple of options here. I can pick some random countries or just pretend I don't know and that I haven't tried. If I do that Granddad will tell me I am lame and that I'm "everything wrong with my generation." If I do try and I get it wrong he will get increasingly triumphant and smug with every wrong answer.

Basically, unless I get very lucky, I can't win.

"Is it Ghana?" As soon as I say it I know it's wrong.

Granddad grins from ear to ear. "No!! That's red, yellow, and green with a big star on it! There's people on the moon that know that, young lady! Go west a bit."

I go west a bit in my head. "Is it . . . Morocco?"

Granddad nearly pulls his own head off doing a big tutting eye-roll thing. "That's going north of Ghana and that's another flag with a star on it! Do they only teach you about countries that have constellations on them these days? I don't know, there's information at your fingertips and none of you bother to learn anything! What if there's a zombie apocalypse, Millie, and all this technology goes off?"

If there's a zombie apocalypse, I don't think my main concern is going to be about learning the flags of other nations. It's going to be about learning how to run exceptionally fast and what mushrooms I can pick in the forest without accidentally poisoning myself.

There is no point explaining this to Granddad. He is clearly desperate to be right and to tell me the answer AND I am clearly going to cheat next time he asks me anything—and learn to lie better.

"It was Belize! That's an easy one, Millie. Know your world. It's the best flag in the known universe. Good phrase on it, too—'Under the Shade I Flourish'! Nice phrase for one of your beauty films that you do. Give people a warning about the dangers of tanning."

I don't do beauty vlogging. Granddad knows this. He's just trying to wind me up. He thinks only-children need to be teased as they miss out on what siblings would do to "harden them up." We are talking about someone born BEFORE TELEVISION (or something). You have to make allowances.

I try a different tactic.

"No way is Belize the best flag!" I say very firmly. "Everyone agrees that Nepal is. It's not even square! And what about Bhutan?! THERE'S A DRAGON ON IT!"

I have learned all the flags of Asia, so I beat Granddad in arguments. I don't know the flags of Africa, but Granddad has lots of time inside these days. He's got time to be a spectacular font of all flag knowledge.

While Granddad and I are arguing about the best flag in the world

(IT IS NEPAL, THOUGH, SERIOUSLY!), I notice a very scary thing out of the corner of my eye.

A cheesecake.

A cheesecake is not just a cheesecake in our family. It is a safety pillow for your heart. If you are emotionally falling through the air (I don't think I can get Danny's sky-diving granny out of my head), a cheesecake will soften the blow. If it's bought from a store, things are bad. If it's Granddad's key lime special, then there's almost certainly a catastrophe looming around the crumbly biscuit base.

And let me tell you, the cheesecake looks VERY green from here.

Granddad can see that I have spotted it. I look at him and ask, "Is everything okay?"

Granddad makes the face that adults make when things are very much NOT OKAY, but they think telling you things are FINE will make terrible things totally simple.

"Fine!" Granddad says completely unconvincingly.

We are in trouble. It is now official. If I didn't know that the flag belonged to Belize, I would think Aunty Teresa had declared independence as a one-woman state and her personal zoo had just been ordered off exoticpets4U.com.

My dad tumbles into the room. He stops dead when he sees me.

"Oh, hi! Erm. Do you want to come and sit down?"

Masses of sugar, mega-carbs, and no standing up? This one *must* be bad.

"I've got something to tell you, Millie," my dad says. "Don't worry. It's all good! It's just a small adjustment to everyday life!"

Dad looks down. It is not all good. Your mouth can tell lies, but your body cannot. This is what detectives in murder shows completely rely on. You touching your ear, you looking down, your right leg twitching a bit—it all says MASSIVE GUILT.

I sit down, and Granddad cuts me a slice of cake. Not a slice; he cuts me a quarter of the cake. It thuds into my dish like a creamy landslide of doom.

"The thing is," Dad says quietly, "I've got the opportunity of a lifetime. It's running a karaoke bar and having a part share in it, too!"

Perhaps I've got it all wrong. This is actually phenomenal news for Dad. He's been looking for full-time work for ages and I know that he'll . . .

"The thing is, it's not here. It's in Ibiza."

Oh. I got it right. My dad is leaving. AGAIN. And just when I thought I'd got him back.

Sometimes, at moments like this, my whole body has this thing where it can buffer entire chunks of information. My mouth decides it's not needed and I go completely silent. I think about what has just been said. Slowly.

- Dad.
- Who has never been around much.
- Is going away AGAIN.
- Just when I am doing something that should make him really proud. Something different. Something that shows him that I've grown up a bit.
- And I've dealt with parts of my anxiety, which used to mainly leave me in a corner somewhere or in my Zen Loo.
- This is not fair. Or right. And I should be used to it, but I am not.

Suddenly my emotional coma ends. I get very angry, and have a brain blurt. Everything comes out. It's a full-on emotional projectile spew.

"Why, Dad? Why would you do this? Why would you choose to listen to people singing Katy Perry songs very badly ALL NIGHT rather than be here with me? It does NOT seem to me to be a good reason to leave your daughter AGAIN. And Ibiza is hours away!"

"It's only a few hours!" Dad semi-shouts.

"It's a few hours IN A PLANE, Dad! It's not like just getting on a bus with some fries!"

At this point my granddad decides that he wants to remind me that you shouldn't eat food on public transport as it can make other people feel "very ill" and that, frankly, he'd ban hot food on planes, too. This is a completely unnecessary thing to say when your own dad has decided he's abandoning you JUST as you were getting a bit closer again. Granddad realizes this and shrinks a bit. I stare at him with a sort of look that tries to encompass all the things that I'm feeling, but it just ends up in a grimace that probably looks rather frightening, I can tell, as Granddad slams another piece of cheesecake on my plate. I now have more cheesecake than it's possible to eat in one sitting. To be fair I could normally very easily polish all of it off, but not now. My stomach is doing a full roller-coaster thing.

Dad continues. "You're back at Mum's house. You're settled. You've even got your own career. How do you think it makes ME feel seeing that my own daughter can create a better business than me?"

This makes me burn red ALL OVER.

"Are you saying that you are going to have to leave the country because I've managed to do something good?"

At this point, just when I thought things couldn't get any worse, Aunty Teresa explodes into the room, comes over, and nearly suffocates me with one of her bear hugs.

Teresa bleats, "I understand, Millie. I understand what it's like to have a dad who doesn't fully support you!"

This starts another argument between Granddad and Teresa. She tries to claim that she couldn't make her ghost tours or her ice cream van work because Granddad wasn't fully behind them. This isn't fair. Granddad has always let his kids do their own thing. He just rightly pointed out that Teresa's haunted "Ice Scream" dessert idea was the worst idea ever, as no one on earth wants to try vampire flavor with a squirt of chili sauce.

Eventually, Dad yells, "Right, EVERYONE needs to calm down!"

This sets me off again. "Why should we be calm because YOU say so?! You play 'Dad' when you want to, and then you're off again. And I put up with it because what else can I do, and I'm—"

"Emotionally sophisticated for your age," Teresa interrupts.

"Er. Yes," I reply. To be honest, I'm not sure I am, but I don't care right now. "But I'm not happy about it. In fact—"

Suddenly Granddad taps a dessert spoon very loudly on the cheese-cake dish. He shouts, "RIGHT! Let's ALL stop and think a minute before we ALL say something that we'll regret! Teresa, I've done nothing but support you. What you just said isn't fair at all, girl."

Teresa slumps in the armchair. "Nothing I do goes right. It's not your fault, Dad. Even the Breakfast Calzones failed. I thought they were a dead certainty. Who wouldn't want egg, sausage, bacon, and ketchup in one convenient folded fried pizza thing at six a.m.?"

Teresa is deadly serious. I'm thinking probably quite a few people.

"The point is, Millie," my dad says as he tries to get back to the point, "all our schemes have sort of come to nothing, and we need jobs that pay. Proper jobs! Real businesses that are viable and can WORK!"

"I'm going to retrain," Teresa announces, "as a paramedic or a nurse. I'm doing a first aid course first. You know. The basics. Cuts. Scrapes. Then I'll go on to the harder stuff. Restarting brains and hearts and what to do if someone is bitten by a rabid squirrel. I was going to try to be a doctor, but I don't think I'm up to it."

Aunty Teresa managed to kill a cactus that an expert in plants had previously described as indestructible. I don't know if this is the right move for her or if I'm being a bit mean.

Granddad sighs. "I'm not getting any younger. My children could do with some growing up a bit!" No, he's not getting any younger, but he doesn't seem to be getting any older either. He should probably do a skincare vlog. Bar some creases around his eyes, he looks about fifty.

Dad does his forced smiley thing. "By doing this, Millie, I can provide for your future. For your education. You'll want to go to university. That doesn't cost peanuts. This cheesecake is wonderful by the way, Dad!"

"Forget the flipping cheesecake!" This is how angry I still am— dessert has become completely irrelevant. "I don't have to go to college. You've done okay!"

Dad looks sad and chases his food around the plate. "Oh, Millie. No, I haven't. I'm living with my dad! I couldn't even get a rental. I've got nothing to show for my life except for a suitcase of mainly neon clothes and lots of very rare vinyl."

I think that makes my dad sound very cool, but I accept that you can't live off your music collection. Especially when you are old. Perhaps I am being really selfish. Everyone has the right to pursue their dreams. Even parents. I should grow up a bit, too, really. I've coped without Dad before. I've coped without him being around for most of my life.

Dad brightens up. "Look, Millie, you are getting to the age where you can come out and see me. We'll have a ball! You can do some karaoke. Bring Lauren!"

At this point Dad starts singing something I've never heard of in my life about jumping around. Teresa joins in.

I give Dad a hug. I'd rather listen to karaoke than do karaoke and that's saying something. I've heard Aunty Teresa try to sing Lady Gaga's "Poker Face." A lot of people did need medical attention after that. Perhaps she could create her own patients. Sing to them and then treat them after, when they are in a critical ear condition.

I always make lousy jokes when I'm feeling blue. Get a grip, Millie.

#LettingPeopleGo

When I get home, it's very quiet. Too quiet. I want to talk to Mum about Dad leaving, but there's lots of angry whispering for some reason. Dave is sitting on the bookcase pretending to read all the titles. She has a sixth sense when it comes to human arguments. She gets out of the way and hides between the *Encyclopedia of the Oceans* (squid are evil) and the *Pop-Up Guide to Dinosaurs* (Mum had it as a kid. It's HUGE and out of date. It doesn't mention the comet that finished them all off).

Comets. Don't think about comets that wipe out entire species, Millie. Not just before bed.

I need to talk to someone.

Getting a signal isn't as hard these days. Mum has souped up the wireless and gone on a decent plan. This is partly because of me and partly because she's realized there's loads of documentaries about the Royal Family available online. She goes to sleep watching *The Crown*. She's trying to work out what season Prince Harry is going to become involved. Never, NEVER say a bad word about Harry and Meghan in this house. You will get a full twenty-minute talk on how they are everything the Royal Family has ever needed. Mum defends Prince Harry with more passion than she defends me. If he vlogged from this house, she'd build him a studio.

That is not me trying to say that Prince Harry would ever be a guest on my vlog, by the way, but I know Mum hopes that this will happen.

I decide this is the perfect time to vlog. Loads of people don't have their dads around. I'm not unusual. This is the sort of stuff that lots of subscribers (and potential subscribers!) understand and it could easily go viral.

I feel bad for saying that, but it's true.

I stop in front of the bookcase. I remember what Lydia Portancia said: "Lots of Dave." I need Dave for three reasons. First, I love her. Second, let's be honest, some people watch the vlog just for her. Third . . .

Lydia Portancia really scares me. That's the truth.

Whatever, I need Dave.

The old treats don't always work with Dave anymore. I creep downstairs and get some tuna in super-thick creamy mayonnaise. Dave goes crazy. Of course, she can read. She knows what she's about to get. Dave follows me upstairs to my room and follows me to my desk. I open the can of tuna and put it in the corner. Dave goes to dive for it but I scoop her up in my arms and hold her tight to me.

I put the phone on and begin to record.

Okay. Hello. Funny time to be talking, but I've just heard a bit of a bombshell. Basically Hashtag Help, my dad is off AGAIN!

So tonight, my dad told me he was going to live abroad and I'm gutted. Really GUTTED because he's only just got back and now he's leaving again. We've never really lived together for long but I was really enjoying him being part of my life again. I get it, but. . . .

At this point Dave has had enough of being patient and attempts to punch me in the chin. I let her go immediately. You can't argue with her. Especially not when she has her claws fully extended. Currently, to her, I am torturing her with gourmet foods. She's had enough. She wants out.

Sorry, I'll be honest with you. There's a can of tuna over there and Dave likes a late cheeky snack. Well, we all do really, don't we?

But . . . my dad's going for all the right reasons. He can't get a job here and he's got the opportunity of a lifetime. It's HARD but the—I know, I hate saying it—SENSIBLE side of me says it's the right thing to do.

And as you've just seen with Dave, you can't hold things back from exploring new opportunities or from tins of tuna in a creamy mayonnaise. You've got to let people do what they think is right for them, I suppose. Whether that's karaoke bars in Ibiza or seafood.

At this point Dave, world-record speed-eater of processed fish, comes back. She doesn't look very impressed. She probably feels with a tin she is slumming it, but she jumps onto my lap and starts purring. I can tell she blatantly wants more food, but I pretend she loves me. Cat owners have to do this a lot.

> **As Dave has just proved, if you love someone set them free, and they will come back to you.**

Dave runs off again. Probably when she realized she's very unlikely to get more food. I look at the camera, semi-exasperated.

> **Eventually she'll come back. You just have to trust it.**
> **Anyway, that's me today. Feeling a bit sad and unhappy.**
> **Leave your comments below, and if you are going through something that's similar, big love to you. It's hard, isn't it?**

At this point Dave flies across the screen. There is no reason for this except to demonstrate that she can still climb up a curtain and rappel down venetian blinds after a big meal.

I upload the video and then hit the sack. Dave snuggles next to me. She has the worst breath in the history of the world—worse than a vlogger who's just on her way to meet her agent for the first time. Mum and Gary have now stopped trying to be quiet and are having a loud chat about something. I think about everything I've done recently—good and bad. No, it can't be anything to do with me. I've obeyed all the crumb rules and I've brushed Dave regularly. I was always carefree with biscuits till Gary arrived. Eating a cookie near him is a military operation. Engage plate, position mouth so nothing spills from the scene of the biscuit, eat, and, finally, observe your surrounding area for any debris that has occurred from you causing structural damage to the biscuit.

Mum and Gary's "discussion" teeters on the brink of a MASSIVE row, but Mum brings it back to a stern, hushed whisper again. I strain to hear what it's all about, but McWhirter starts doing his cleaning thing and I can't hear a word of what is being said downstairs.

As soon as Dave hears the robot vacuum, she jumps off me for a ride. She uses my arm as a vault and decides to use her claws for extra stability as she leaps. This makes me yelp loudly. Very loudly. I can tell it's loud, as Mum clearly hears it over everything and the next thing I know she is in my bedroom checking that I am "not dying."

She is angry.

"Millie! Please do not make that noise again. I've got enough going on without you overreacting to a slight scratch!"

I defend myself. "It isn't a slight scratch!"

Mum shouts, "Go to sleep! I don't want to hear anything else from you for the rest of the day. Night, I mean. Whatever—just please stay quiet. Now, hello! I mean—good night!"

And with that, Mum disappears out the door. I have no chance to tell her that Dad is leaving, that I'm upset, that the whole world is shifting on its axis again AND NO ONE SEEMS TO CARE (I know they do, really) but COME ON, EVERYONE!

Why is it when you want your parents to be around they aren't, and when you don't want them in your face they are?

#Frenemies

When I wake up the next morning, I'm blind. This is because Dave is lying over my eyes. She's overexhausted after doing stunts on McWhirter and has decided she likes to be a living eye mask—the unhelpful, nonbeauty kind. The house feels odd. Mum and Neat Freak Gary are creatures of routine, but that's all gone out the window today. For a start, showers don't last for the right amount of time. Most of my morning routine has to be based around Gary's twenty-two-minute cleansing ritual. This morning, that doesn't seem to happen. I can tell by the lack of washing-up that breakfast hasn't been eaten by anyone, and that includes Dave. No one has given her food. She is very angry and gnaws at my ankles. I'm nearly late for school because of all this. Other people are my natural alarm clock.

I'm also late because Lydia Portancia has already sent me something about the vlog.

> Millie!
> Fantastic response! Emotional subject matter beautifully picked and elaborated on by you! Vulnerability means viral! You know how to get people going! And Dave's incredible

73

as ever! I wonder though if you've ever considered upping
your production value? A little makeup? Nothing that isn't
"you," of course, but something that just enhances your
intrinsic brand values and your lovely face. Have a think
and get back to me by the end of the day.

KV!

LP x

This e-mail makes me feel sick, so I put it in the part of my trained brain that's called "Try to forget about it and panic later." I rush into school. Lauren runs up to me. "Meltdown to the last vlog, Mills!"

"Meltdown" is Lauren's way of saying that things have gone really well.

"I haven't had time to look," I tell her. "Dave was trying to kill me!"

Lauren's eyes go really wide. "Mills, SERIOUSLY vlog about that! Pets that try to kill!"

Lauren can sometimes take things a bit literally.

"Not really, Lauren," I reassure her. "I'm just joking!"

Lauren can't let go of the idea now, though. "People do love murder stuff, though! They love, like, a gruesome twist on things. I watched this thing once where a woman poisoned her husband slowly over months with weed killer. A bit at a time. It was famous. Now, the manufacturers have to put something in it to make you vomit so no one can be poisoned by weed killer again! You could do a podcast serial. 'My Cat Is a Killer.' She puts poison on her paws and then shoves them in your face."

Even for Lauren, this is a bit odd. Everyone is acting strange today. Perhaps there is a full moon. I try to get her back on planet Earth.

"Do you ever get that feeling . . ."

74

Lauren interrupts me. "Your dad! Millie, I'm so sorry about your dad going. Sorry, I just got a bit preoccupied with Frenemy Psycho Cats."

Lauren puts her arm around me. I let her, but when people are sweet to me after something bad has happened, THAT'S when I really want to cry. I don't, though. Crying at school is still a no-no.

"Thanks, Loz. It's not just that, though. The whole house was weird this morning. I don't think Mum knows yet either. Perhaps she does, but I'm sure she would have mentioned it. It just felt a bit bizarre."

"In what way?" Lauren asks.

"I don't know. It just seemed like something big was happening." I sigh. "It's probably nothing. You know what my head is like. It can make something out of nothing. It can turn a tiny event into something that is actually not happening at all."

Honestly, I think vlogging may have made this trait worse.

Lauren nods. "Yes, you can turn a perfectly brilliant cat into a potential death trap."

This makes me laugh. "But there was something weird going on. I haven't made that bit up."

Lauren looks sad. "I totally believe you but, to be honest, Mills, my house has always felt like that. Psychologists call it my norm. I've seen it on TV. Chaos is my standard."

I try to cheer her up.

"But it's better these days, isn't it?"

Lauren sighs. "Yeah, now that my parents have admitted that they will never be getting back together and actually they can't stand each other, things have certainly improved."

This is one of those things that is simultaneously happy and terrible and a relief all in one. I don't really know what to say, so I give Lauren a huge hug. Lauren knows I'm stuck and says, "Anyway, we need to hurry up or we're going to be late for class!"

I tell her I just need to fix myself up and go to the bathroom. Yes, feeding the animal you are responsible for is important, but so is brushing your hair.

Once I'm in the bathroom, I look in the mirror. I have dark circles under my eyes and a large cat injury on my arm. I do not look my best, but I'll do. I say this to myself as it's important for your mouth to give your brain reassurance: "Millie. You will do!"

Just as I'm making this declaration, I notice that someone is smiling in the mirror behind me.

It's Erin. *Former* enemy, now . . .

Now, I don't know what she is, and I can't get a thought out of my head. Lydia Portancia's e-mail pops up from the "panic later" part of my head, What Erin *could* be hits me straight in the sensible part of my brain. Or the ambitious, focused, completely-intent-on-success part of my brain. I can't decide what it is and if it's good. Also, I don't have time to decide.

#Bathroom Negotiations

Erin corners me by the sinks. These days, it's not really cornering. It's more a cuddly surrounding.

I feel embarrassed. I don't like people catching me doing my personal pep talks. They are for my ears and eyes only.

"Millie, your latest vlog was so raw and incredible."

Erin is in full compliment mode. It's very hard to trust this. I fact, I still do not trust this.

"Was it?" I say. "Thank you!"

"Yeah," Erin continues, "I just love how you manage to make the really emotional stuff funny, you know, with Dave? It's a really tough thing to carry off, but you totally seem to manage it."

"Thanks!" I say. Again. I'm still not good at the whole praise thing. It makes me feel prickly. Especially with Erin. She used to be the queen of the backhanded compliment. What she gave with one hand, she took away with the other, and then poured a bucket of ice water over your head. Not actually, but on Instagram. That's who she was.

Who she is now is someone who could help me do what Lydia wants. I KNOW THAT SOUNDS TERRIBLE, but it's TRUE.

"Erin. I had an e-mail this morning from my agent and she thinks

I could do with looking more professional to up my brand values. And I wondered if, perhaps . . ."

I can't believe I'm saying this.

". . . you'd like to help me do my makeup for my vlog?"

Erin basically leaps in the air and nearly slips on a paper towel. Even when she has an accident, she still looks glam.

"Millie, seriously, I'd LOVE to. I think I could just make your vlog feel a touch more polished. You're professional already. Just more together as a product. Nothing too heavy. I do understand light and flattering angles and filters. NOT that you need them. I think you'd get even more subscribers. Truly I do."

Erin is very convincing and seems really sincere. I try to be honest.

"What's worrying me is I'm not a makeup vlog. I don't think all that contouring stuff is really me. I'm about the real stuff, not . . . fake stuff."

I can't believe I'm talking to Erin like this. She used to be terrifying. Now she's just another girl in a bathroom trying to have a conversation over the sound of a hand dryer.

Erin tries to comfort me. "I can still make you look like you! Just a better you."

A horrible thought goes through my head. What if Erin makes me look incredibly terrible? The sort of terrible that I won't notice but when other people see me I will look like a clown. Not even a happy clown. A terrifying, living-in-the-drain sort of evil clown.

No. That's Old Erin. This is New Erin. Wise and improved and—no, I still don't trust her.

"I really appreciate this, Erin. I'll e-mail my agent and get back to you."

I'll e-mail my agent and get back to you? Who do I think I am?! A Kardashian?!

Erin stares hard at me. "Sure!" she says breezily. "You know where to find me. I'm around."

Erin glides out and I type a quick reply to Lydia. I can't wait till the end of the day. My agent feels like a huge thundercloud following me constantly overhead.

Hello Lydia,
I think I've found someone that can help me with looking
more pro.
Thanks
Erin x

I fire it off, feel good about how I'm handling everything, and then realize I haven't even signed the e-mail with my own name.

I have never been so grateful to go to chemistry class in my entire life. Hurrah for atoms and molecules, they have got me out of being a total spoon and they get me in to seeing Danny.

#BradleyBreak

Danny is not in class today. I message him to ask him where he is, but get no response. To be honest, I'm a bit hurt. I thought after seeing my vlog he would immediately want to speak to me. He's either seen my vlog and can't cope with me being emotional (this is my anxiety talking, I don't actually think this is the case for one minute), OR he is too busy with his big family meeting to have looked at what is going on with me. Perhaps his grandma has decided she wants to scale Mount Everest or something and they are trying to talk her out of it. I don't think they should. As far as I'm concerned, old women can do what they like. They come from a time when women had fewer opportunities! If they want to travel and probably injure themselves rappelling in the snow I think they should be allowed to!

Allowed to? I check myself. They don't need permission either! Just do it, old ladies. We are with you!

Sometimes I vlog in my head. That was a great example of it. It's good practice and it stops me from being a pathetic girlfriend.

At break time, I spend my time in the quiet corners of school. It saves me from live human vlog reaction. Lots of people want to make appointments to meet Dave. Sometimes it feels like too much. Kayla

Beacham, who has her own gluten-free snack business and should be on *The Apprentice*, is already talking to me about "merch opportunities" like #LoveDave environmentally friendly bags. Etsy isn't the answer to everything. There are already Dave pages on Pinterest, too.

The quiet corners mean I bump into Bradley. He likes to get away from noise of any kind. He's sitting on concrete steps doing some kind of really detailed drawing. I go up to him.

"Hello, Bradley. How's . . ."

Bradley shoots his hand up in the air and wiggles it. This means "give me time." I stand there and wait. He's not being rude. He's just being Bradley.

Eventually he stops. "Sorry," he says quietly, "I was just doodling a lift mechanism to show my subscribers. It's a revolutionary design. They think it can go sideways like a classic paternoster, but without the risk of death. Which is good, as in my experience, death does sort of curtail your ability to have fun. Anyway, how are you? I was sorry to hear about your dad going. That's, er—well, that just sucks."

Bradley sort of always says it like it is. It's very sweet that he watches my vlog. It's even sweeter that he tries to make me feel better.

He looks at me earnestly. "Has fame changed your life, Millie?"

Fame. I try not to think about it too much. "It's not really fame, is it, though?" I sigh. "I'm not in a private jet with an entourage. I'm still me. I'm just me with people looking at my life and being interested in my life."

Bradley laughs. "Yeah, I think you'll find lots of people would define that as a celebrity!"

I can't think about that too much. I need my Zen Loo. The tiled, pine-clean, disinfected place of calm and safety. I need to just breathe and rearrange the jumble in my head. I've got ways to cope and one of them is sometimes by blocking out actual reality in a tiny cubicle. A big part of me doesn't feel like I deserve any of this.

I can tell Bradley anything. I trust him and, honestly, he still hasn't got many close friends. He doesn't really need them. He says he'd rather have a "few humans that mean something than lots of the same species who mean nothing at all." That's just the way he talks. This is someone with a hugely successful lift and escalator vlog. He knows what he is doing.

I sit down beside him. I can't lie to him.

"If I'm being honest with you, Bradley, I mainly have increased anxiety levels. I find myself vlogging in my head sometimes."

"Oh, I do that!" snaps Bradley. "I wouldn't worry too much."

"But is it healthy?" I ask.

Bradley stares off into the distance. He seems to think for a while. Bradley often takes a long time to answer questions. He thinks about them, then puts them in a specific compartment in his brain that asks questions about questions.

"I think people have always vlogged in their heads. In a way. They imagine talking to people who aren't there. They imagine conversations they are going to have or conversations they don't want to have. They daydream. Prehistoric man probably vlogged in a way in their own heads."

I look at Bradley strangely. "What would they vlog about?"

Bradley grins from ear to ear. "Oh, you know, the everyday stuff!" (And Bradley puts on a caveman sort of voice.) "Have seen a mastodon. It big. Shall I try to fit it in sandwich?"

At this point Bradley collapses in fits of laughter at his own joke.

I try to get him back to the point.

"They didn't have delis till the Iron Age, Bradley. Everyone knows that."

Unfortunately, this makes Bradley crack up even more. I have to let him shake with the giggles until his sensible side kicks back in. Eventually, he comes around and sees that I'm still looking a bit tense.

"Sorry, Millie," he says sheepishly. "I'd try to just . . . enjoy it more. I think you are coping with it fine. You're still the same old Millie. Is Romeo able to handle it?"

By "Romeo" Bradley means Danny. I can tell Bradley still feels weird about him.

"Yes!" I snap a bit defensively. "He's actually very supportive of everything I do!"

Bradley looks at me like he's not convinced.

"I think you have to be a vlogger to truly get vlogging. You have to understand what it takes to connect with people. He doesn't strike me as our type. He'll say stuff like, 'I prefer the real world,' like what we do isn't real and all fake. I can't stand people like that. They think they are revolutionary. Same old thing—just trying to be cool by making out that they are different. They don't know what it means to be *actually* different. I bet he's never been called a nerd because he appreciates a good speed governor."

Though this is a bit of a rant, Danny HAS said things like that, but NO WAY can I tell Bradley that. First, it feels disloyal, and second, I think Bradley might be—

Hang on.

"What's a speed governor, Bradley?"

Bradley looks at me like I'm insane.

"It governs the speed of the elevator. The clue's in the name, Millie."

I realize I look a bit spoon, so I change the subject.

"Danny hasn't said anything like that. Not really. He just prefers sports."

Bradley makes a face of disgust. "Odd thing, sports. Being out of breath. Broken bones. Spending your entire life on a racetrack or a field for the first twenty years on this earth just to win a medal. Then what? Nothing. You have to retire at thirty and watch other people become better at what you love. Sports are total madness, Millie. I'd ban them."

There's not a lot I can say to this. Bradley seems to get very angry about lots of things. Perhaps it's hormonal. Perhaps boys have a time of the month. I try to offer a positive thought.

"Carb-loading is good!"

Bradley looks at me down his glasses. "You can do that and lose the running about. Perfection."

Then, and don't ask me why, my mind decides to take the brain bus to a really weird stop.

"I've asked Erin to do my makeup."

Bradley tenses up for a moment, then relaxes his shoulders and almost shrugs.

"Great idea!" he says. "She helped me with my new, slightly improved look." Bradley almost swaggers. He knows he looks good. It's annoying. I change the subject back to me.

"The thing is, my agent suggested it, and I can see what she means, but I don't want to be all about how I look, Bradley. The whole glamorous, flouncy girl thing isn't really me. What if I lose a lot of followers?!"

Bradley does his intense thing. "You've got to do what you like, Millie. Erin helped me, but she didn't try to take over. I think she's learned her lesson. She's been horrible in the past, and she's hurt my feelings, but other people have done that, too. I've forgiven them and moved on, so why not her?"

I know Bradley means me, but it's different. I didn't go out to hurt him. Erin was just plain evil to everyone. The whole school agrees. If there were a vote about it, there'd be a record turnout and everyone would be voting YES to still leave Erin WELL alone. And I know when Lauren finds out that I've asked Erin to do my makeup, she'll be FURIOUS.

I can't say any of this, so I just say to Bradley, "Thank you."

As Bradley leaves, he turns around and winks at me. My stomach flips a bit. Pancake feelings. Actually, more pancakes being carried by butter-flies riding on bikes on a really bumpy road. This isn't good. I should have wink resistance. Eye movements should not make me remotely wobbly. I am Millie Porter. I am as tough as a very tough thing that's had, of late, a very tough time.

I bury my emotions by demolishing an apple I find in the bottom of my bag. I can't remember putting it in there. Probably Dave rolled it in there. She's always putting stuff in . . .

I stop eating the apple. Having a cat that helps you with your lunch isn't always pleasant. Dave kills cockroaches with those paws.

#Bears

When Dave wants feeding, she either attacks you or does this weird thing where she sits about half an inch from your face and stares at you. In the back of my head, all during the morning, Erin is doing both of these things in my head. Since the chat with Bradley I can't get her out of my mind.

She's still there when I sit down to eat lunch. Lauren joins me. She's still full-moon crazy—even for her. I try to take my mind off my . . . mind by chatting about just about anything else. You can tell how desperate I am to do this as I decide to talk about classes.

"Have you done your history homework?" I ask Lauren. We had to imagine being a resistance fighter in a war. I spent ages on mine.

Lauren proudly pulls her work out of the bag. "I have done it!" she declares. "And I've done it with a twist!"

Lauren's twists on anything can be either total genius or madness. There is no in-between.

"The twist, Millie, is I am a resistance fighter, BUT I'm not actually human. I'm a bear."

Even for Lauren this is bizarre.

Lauren can see I'm completely confused and explains.

"Millie! A bear fought in World War Two in the Polish army. It's a true fact. Google it!"

Lauren can see I'm still wearing my WHAT THE HELL face. This is a serious subject.

"It's simple," Lauren says. "I've done the whole resistance thing from the perspective of an animal. Basically, I hate the enemy, I've got huge paws, and I can still smell a picnic from miles away."

This makes me laugh, but I immediately feel guilty.

"I don't think you should make a joke out of a major global conflict, Lauren."

Now it's Lauren's turn to look confused.

"I'm not! I'm SERIOUS," she shouts. "I'm just trying to do something a bit different. The teacher is going to see the same essay about thirty times. I just want people to know that animals fight in things that humans create, too! Think of *War Horse*—this could actually become a classic!"

I very much doubt this, but I don't tell her that. I just say, "I think the picnic thing sounds a bit . . . funny."

"You've got to be authentic to bears," Lauren snaps. I decide to leave it there because when she's in a mood like this, you cannot convince her.

"Tell you what," she whispers, "Dave would be a terrible animal soldier. You couldn't tell her what to do. She'd just walk off. That reminds me—have you checked the vlog reaction yet?"

No, I haven't. I used to check it immediately. Sometimes I still do. Other times I squirrel myself away from it. It's a mental mood thing. I usually like to do it when I'm on my own and I can just take everything in. Especially when it's about something like my dad leaving. It's too emotional to have a real live audience.

My dad is leaving. I'm getting my head around it—but in real life, not vlog life. I need more time.

What with Bradley, Erin, and Lauren's rebel bear I'd completely forgotten all about it.

My phone vibrates. It's a message from Erin. It's a photo of someone who looks totally incredible but it also looks like they are wearing no makeup at all. It's fantastic. A work of art.

With it Erin has written:

> **The look I did for my cousin, I'd use with you. Natural. Know you don't like fake. E x**

I exhale very hard.

"Who was that?" Lauren asks. She's suspicious. We know each other so well that she can read my breathing sounds. She can tell that I've just received something that's left me in a bit of a mess.

"Oh, no one," I say. "Seriously, I'm just . . . just . . . just looking at comments."

Lauren peers at me through a crumpled-up face. "Millie, when you do a stutter thing I know you are lying."

I can't tell Lauren that I'm speaking to Erin. Erin made Lauren a global laughingstock after she couldn't walk in high heels. Me speaking to Erin is like the Polish Army bear defecting to the enemy for a nice piece of cake.

"No, Lauren, honestly," I say quickly, "my brain is just buffering all the messages I've got."

Lauren picks up her tray. "You know, I'm your best friend. You can tell me anything."

"I know, Lauren, and I love you for it! Seriously, there's nothing wrong!"

Lauren disappears to the bathroom, leaving me to wonder if I'm the worst person on earth. Is it terrible to go behind Lauren's back? She'll find out. OR would I be terrible for not giving Erin a second chance? Bradley is right—we DO all vlog in our heads naturally.

Bradley is also right about something else. Erin knows what she is doing, and the sooner I get her on board the better.

I message her back.

Talent! Shall we try to do something together?

I'm just picking up my lunchbox when my phone goes off again. It's Erin. She messages back immediately.

Love to! What time would work?

I look around the cafeteria. It's like she's spying on me. I decide to reply later. I need a delay to give me a bit of text power.

I think I've agreed to Erin coming around my house. *Erin!*

Not so long ago, it would have been preferable to let Lauren's rebel bear in the house.

#Drama

When I get home, Mum is doing angry ironing. She's attack-ing a shirt with steam on level-three heat. This is never a good sign. Dave is nowhere to be seen. She would have seen Mum doing this and gone straight behind the couch. It's Dave's panic room.

When Mum sees me, though, she stops everything, rushes over, and hugs me. She won't let me go.

"Oh, Millie! I'm so sorry about your dad. I saw your vlog. I screamed at him on the phone. He didn't tell me! I mean, I'm not saying he shouldn't have told you first, but he should have told me, too! Total strangers saw before me! It had thousands of views before I went near it! In fact, why didn't you tell me last night?! This is typical of him. He's got a heart of gold, but he's totally useless. BUT you can go and see him! WE can! Me and you. Just me and you."

To be honest, I'm very surprised at this reaction. My mum and my dad have always gotten along, but I didn't think she missed him or wanted to be with him in any way. She seems more upset than me.

I finally get out of her bear hug (ever since Lauren went on about the bear I'm thinking of them ALL the time) and it's then I realize that her eyes are all red and puffy.

"Are you okay?" I ask her.

"Yeah, I'll be fine in no time!"

When Mum does this rubbish rhyme, it means she is not fine at all.

My mum doesn't like being not all right. She is old school. She likes to keep all the feelings under the carpet. Because of this, she makes me go upstairs to change out of my school uniform. It gives her some breathing space. I get straight into my pajamas. It's the only way to be after school. I lie on my bed and make myself look at the comments on my vlog.

There are lots and loads of new subscribers, which gives me a bit of head-spin, a rush of pride, and desire to vomit all at once.

I look at the most liked.

Honest and Dave is everything.

(Yes, and yes she is. I don't tell her that but she is incredible.)

Sorry about your dad. My dad did this, too. We don't know where he is. Happened 4 years ago.

(That's awful. Luckily, my dad keeps in touch and he does send cards.)

Make sure you keep in touch. Sometimes going abroad means disappearing forever.

(It won't.)

U R lucky 2 have a dad in the first place. Count your blessing.

(I think that should be plural, but never mind—and yes, I know I am.)

Typical drama queen. Making something out of nothing to get hits.

(This is horrible, but is it also a bit true? I knew a ton of people wouldn't "get" it.)

Is Dave drugged?

(WHAT?! OF COURSE NOT! DAVE IS THE LOVE OF MY LIFE. I WOULD NEVER HURT HER.)

Another subscriber replies.

How can you drug a cat?

(THANK YOU! Of course, you can't. Unless you are a twisted evil vet and I am not!)

I say this out loud but I don't comment. I'm not commenting on anything. It's the safest way.

I read on. Two people are having a full-on argument underneath my vlog.

Of course you can drug cats! Animals should not be made to perform. This is no better than the thousands of dolphins that are in captivity that are

made to jump through hoops to get a fish treat. It's disgusting.

This makes me furious. I go downstairs. Mum is always the person to talk to in situations like this. She's got a level head and she—

Mum is now attacking a pair of pants. It smells like something is burning. I don't think she should iron nylon slacks on a maximum setting. I think they are melting.

I look at her face and decide I am not going to mention this right now. In fact, changing the subject seems like a very good idea.

"Mum, have you ever heard of an animal being drugged so they can do stunts and tricks?"

Mum answers like she is in a dream.

"I think they used to do it in films. You'd need a lot of tranquilizers for an elephant, though. People can be cruel when you don't do what they want you to do."

I go to reassure her. Don't worry, Mum, I'm not going to ever do anything like that to Dave. I mean, she can't even handle catnip.

Suddenly Mum bursts into tears.

This is weird as it's not just a few tears, it's full-on sobbing. For a minute I just stand there with my mouth wide open. Mum folds into a heap in the big chair. Dave appears from behind the sofa and starts licking Mum's tears off her face. Please note—my cat is better in an emergency than me.

Eventually my shock wears off and I manage to give Mum a huge hug.

Mum manages to talk through her tears.

"Millie. Gary and I have split up. He's left."

This is strange. Not so long ago I would have wanted Gary to go. It would have been my absolute dream. He is so difficult to live with. He is super strict, uber-grumpy, and he could sense a speck of dust from four miles away. Now that he's left, I'm honestly sad. This feeling is mainly for Mum, though.

Suddenly, I have a terrible thought.

"Oh no. Was it me coming back to live here?"

My mouth says this thought. It does that sometimes.

Mum reassures me so fast it's scary.

"No! NO!" she cries. "I'll be really straight with you, Millie. Gary wanted to have a baby and I didn't. It's as simple as that. I don't want to do the whole diaper and horrific toddler thing again. I feel way too old. I understand that he does, though, and that's why . . ."

Mum breaks down again, Dave puts her paw on Mum's arm, and I try to say something supportive.

"I'm sorry, Mum. I know you were totally loved up and that he made you happy."

Mum looks at me. "It's not just that, Millie. He's taken the robot vacuum cleaner! It did most of the cleaning! What now? I can't go back to life without it!"

This makes me laugh, but Mum is dead serious.

"It's all the other stuff Gary did, too," Mum says. "Now I'll need a stepladder again to mend the shower light and the bathroom is half tiled. Who's going to do that?!"

This makes me annoyed. I reassure her.

"We can do the tiling! We are feminists!"

Mum sighs. "It's nothing to do with gender equality, Millie. I haven't got the time or the energy to do things like that! I haven't got the money, either. I just want to come home to a clean house, a cooked meal, a decent box set, and someone to share it with. It's not too much to ask, is it?"

"Don't worry!" I say. "There's other people we know who can help. Lauren's dad can do little jobs. His own house is a total disgrace, but he can do DIY. And we can totally get you on Tinder. We'll find you a guy who's good around the house and has a wide range of robot cleaning products. It'll be FINE, Mum."

To be honest, Lauren's dad is a bit of a nightmare. He puts Lauren through a lot, what with arguing with her mum since she was born. Lauren used to dread going home. But my mum needs some help around the house, and he can do it.

With this, Mum gives me a huge hug and says she wants five minutes on her own just to get herself together. She disappears upstairs, probably to keep on crying on her own for a time.

Wow. This is a huge shock. I hate seeing Mum like this. And I understand where she's coming from. I probably could have dealt with having a little sister. It's Mum's choice, though, and honestly, if she'd given birth to a boy I would have moved not just back to Granddad's house but probably to the moon.

The mad, ambitious, maniac part of my brain thinks it might have been great drama for my vlog. "Hashtag Help! My six-month-old brother is the devil," but no, not worth it even for that.

Also, Gary did do some amazing things—Mum is right. McWhirter did most of the dusting without any of us trying and Gary did a lot of great cooking. Him leaving does mean a lot more of Mum's meals. That is not a good thought—appalling leftover pie with lots of fridge debris and her legendary "nachos," aka chips with sour cream, a whole avocado (no attempt at guacamole!), and beans.

I realize I'm being selfish. We'll manage. We did before. When it was just Mum and me it was wonderful. Her heart is broken and I've got to help her. I'll start by making a fuss over her and organizing a good night.

I would normally do a vlog, but when Mum comes back downstairs I suggest the things you absolutely need when a relationship breaks down. Ice cream and a movie.

Mum is quite clear. "Millie. Nothing romantic and nothing about love or teenagers dying in a forest because of an ancient curse they find in a tree or something."

I suggest *Wonder Woman*. She survives. Men die. In fact, men die for her.

Mum winks at me and says, "That sounds like just what I need."

At this point, my phone goes off. It's a message from Danny.

> Hi M. Got a virus or something. Temperature 101 degrees. Mum making me eat soup. Won't be at school for a few days. No voice so can't talk. Just saw your vlog though. Baby, I'm sorry but know you are strong and you look and sound great. Dave also incredible. Try a bit of Zan. D xx

"Try a bit of Zan." I wish I could explain to Danny and lots of other people that it isn't that easy.

Also, I know not being able to speak is a very good excuse for not calling, but I still feel a bit . . .

No, I'm being terrible. He's just ill. Tonight is ALL about my mum and making her feel better. That's what good daughters and good women do—support each other even when they are feeling *bleurgh*.

#Bear Fail

The next day at school, there's still no Danny, and Lauren is furious. She storms up to me at break. I have this terrible feeling that she's found out about me and Erin. Rumors can flash around school very fast. But it's not that. The teacher gave her a fail for her essay featuring the bear. He said it was a "trite way to deal with a serious subject."

"This is everything that is wrong with education!" Lauren rants. "You get punished for having an imagination. There's too much information available. We can go to places of knowledge not previously explored. Teachers need to realize this. Everything is too interesting. Too distracting."

As if on cue, my phone pings and Lydia Portancia sends me ANOTHER distracting message.

> Hello Millie!
> The latest vlog is a triumph! Dave! DAVE! What a natural
> and as ever you were wonderful! Who is Erin BTW? Don't
> change your main brand name. You're not established
> enough to do that yet. I'm talking to some key players and
> media partners and I will have some exciting developments

soon! Perhaps we can even get you on with a psychologist!
Great news about upping production values.

KV

Lydia x

I manage to swipe the phone away from Lauren's prying eyes, but she catches the end of the message over my shoulder. "What does KV stand for?"

"Keep Vlogging. She always says that."

Lauren scrunches her nose up. "That's a bit . . . forced."

I know she's right, but I feel like I should defend Lydia.

"It's just the way she is!" I reply. "She is very upbeat. All the time. I don't want to be like that, though."

Lauren looks at me. "No, I hate people who are always happy. Especially morning people. They are just plain wrong."

"No, I don't mean that," I say quietly. "It's something she's suggested. I don't want to be a Dr. Phil kind of vlog with clever guests using long words. I don't think that's me. I'm not a completely serious thing. This is a truthful and hopefully sometimes helpful to others 'me' vlog with a random cat."

Lauren nods. "Tell Lydia whatsherface that, then!"

I can't tell Lydia whatsherface this, as she terrifies me and I can't tell anyone that as I'll look incredibly tragic.

"Whatever," Lauren continues. "Can we talk about my fail, please? You heard my idea. It was fantastic, Mills. No one else had anything like it."

This makes me pull a face. "Could that be, Loz, because it was a bit silly? I mean, just a tiny bit 'out there.' Rebel bears? Even for you?"

99

Lauren smirks. "Well, *a bit*, but that's what you should do your next vlog on! How to do decent homework in a world full of other more interesting stuff going on. And not just now, but in the past. The concept of time is trying to catch us out constantly. We are all basically the new Doctor Who! Do it about that!"

This isn't a bad idea. I really want to talk about Mum, but I can't talk about Mum (she would go bananas if I shared more of her private life online), and I don't want to talk about Dad anymore. Perhaps something about school would relate to a lot of people. Also, if I do something that's about Lauren, it might soften the Erin blow that is coming.

"I'm going to do it, Lauren, and I'm going to dedicate it to you."

Lauren bursts with pride. "I am happy to be your inspirational figure, Millie, but I must go now as I have to do my history essay again. This time it's got to feature a human."

"Just before you go and just so you know," I say very quickly, "Gary and Mum have split up."

Lauren's eyes pop out and her neck attains a giraffelike length.

"What?!" she squeals.

"I know!" I say. "I can't believe it either. He wanted a baby. She didn't, and that was it!"

"That's a pretty huge thing," Lauren says with a sigh. "Honestly, I think my parents were happier till I came along. They love me. They've always loved me, but I don't think they could juggle romance and a screaming thing."

I give Lauren a massive hug. "They were never meant to be together, Lauren. It's one hundred percent NOT your fault. Don't even think about that."

"Yeah, I know," Lauren sniffs. "Anyway now that they've split up, things are a lot better. Dad is like a new man! It's like he's twenty years younger. He's playing his guitar a lot again. He's quite good!"

This reminds me.

"Do you think your dad would be up for doing a few jobs around our house? Mum could do it, but she doesn't want to. It would be a huge load off her mind!"

"Yeah!" Lauren smiles. "I'll ask him after school. I need to get on now. See you later, Mills."

Lauren runs off, and I begin to think about the new vlog.

Lydia is right. If there were ever a time to experiment with things, it's now. I've got real followers who I think won't mind me looking . . . I can't say great, but BETTER.

I send Erin a text. She's great at what she does and we've all made mistakes in life!

> Going to vlog after school. Want to come to mine and do
> my face?

Erin replies with her usual super speed. It's just a series of thumbs-up and smiley face emojis and the time, 5:00 p.m.?

I reply with another thumbs-up. I hover for a moment over SEND, and then I just go for it. Sometimes you've just got to take a risk.

That's it, then. I'm now a truthful, hopefully helpful vlog with a random diva cat *and* added makeup.

I don't know if I want to be that or not. Is this vlog making me like Snow White's stepmother? Beautiful but all devious and scheming?

#ErinStyle

When I get home Mum isn't back from work. I think she's probably staying longer, as she doesn't want to come home to a house without a Gary and one of his gourmet fish concoctions that he's rustled up from nothing. She is already missing his cooking. Plus, there's already lots of added dust. I clean for a bit, but I don't try to cook anything. I want to cheer Mum up, not make her feel worse or potentially kill her with salmonella. Or botulism. I've googled all the germs. Some of them seem to have faces.

Honestly, I feel quite relieved that she's not around. I don't think she'd appreciate having anyone else here at the moment. I think she wants to, as Granddad would say, lick her wounds like a dog that's had a car crash. This is one of Granddad's favorite sayings. It means sometimes you don't want to see anyone. You just want to hide yourself away in a tiny kennel, be kind to yourself, and pretend that no one else exists. This is a real blow to Mum. She's said a flat no to any dating app. I can't see her having a relationship for a long time. I think she thought Gary was "the one."

At this point, I wonder if Danny is *my* one. I think it's probably a bit early to have met your forever soulmate, but the thought of not having him in my life makes me feel very weird and bad.

I don't have much time to think about this as the doorbell goes at precisely 4:56 p.m. It's like Erin has been hovering outside waiting.

Erin glides in and seems completely at ease. She brings in lots of boxes. One for the face, one for the eyes, one for the lips, one for the cheeks—she is product central. All of it must have cost so much.

I manage to stutter, "I vlog in my room. Shall we do it there?"

Erin nods enthusiastically. In fact, she beams from ear to ear. "Thanks so much for letting me in on this, Millie. I know in the past I was sometimes hideous but, you know, I learned such valuable life lessons that have helped me grow as a person."

This sounds like something from a book and I feel uneasy. It's too late now, though. I put my chair near the window so Erin can have the right light and she begins to work her magic.

Erin doing my makeup is very different to the time that Lauren did it. There's primers, bases, blushes, brows, and things I don't even quite understand. Erin moves effortlessly from one box to another. She won't let me look in the mirror till she's completely finished. Finally, she lets me go to the bathroom to have a look.

WOW.

For the natural look, I do feel like I'm wearing a lot.

My lashes are so long, you could high-dive off them and probably do several somersaults before you hit the carpet. My lips are shiny like aluminum foil. My cheekbones are toothpick sharp. It's all a bit much.

Erin can see that I'm a bit freaked out. "Don't trust the mirror. This is cosmetics for the screen. Look in your phone! That's what all this is designed for."

When I look in the camera I'm blown away. I look incredible, but kind of not "me." It's like looking at Hollywood Millie. Red Carpet

Millie. I feel like my character should sort of adjust to this new face. Which is actually just the face I had on half an hour ago but with loads of stuff on it.

Erin hangs over me like a mantis. I dare not try and change a thing. There's an uncomfortable silence.

Erin grins at all her work (i.e. me) and says, "Well, what do you think?"

I tell her that I think it looks fantastic, which is certainly true.

"I'm going to vlog now," I tell her. "Any chance you can just wait in the lounge while I do it?"

Erin says, "Sure." I wait till she is all the way downstairs before I start. The thought of having Erin as an audience while I vlog makes me feel uncomfortable. I don't think we are friends yet.

I settle myself down in front of my phone. I take a deep breath and vlog . . .

Hi! Millie Porter here.

Just want to talk about homework. It's not a glamorous subject, but Hashtag Help! Lots of us can't concentrate because the universe is NEVER dull. Shout out to my best friend, Lauren, who inspired all this. Love you, Loz. I think a lot of people have the problem that Lauren has. Basically, it's very difficult to do your homework when there's a ton of stuff online that's fascinating. I'm not just talking about looking at your friends' Instagram pages, scrolling through your own timeline or how you can go down a rabbit hole on YouTube. That's standard. I mean, when you google a fact for school that's completely legitimate and then you find out something much more interesting. For example, did you know that the closest living relative to a T. rex is a chicken? That is genuinely more exciting than cell division and percentages. Though both probably played a part in making dinosaurs like poultry.

(I feel more up than normal. It feels like a forced up. I just keep wondering, *what are people going to think?* Relax, Millie. Think of your followers. They just want you. That's what they are here for . . . and Dave. Probably Dave.)

You know what everyone says at this point. *(I do an impression of a nagging mum):* Turn the Wi-Fi off. I am completely incapable of doing that. But I know someone who can do it for me. I am first going to use the T. Rex's nearest living relative: THE CHICKEN!

I pull out a cooked chicken drumstick that I got from the fridge. Mum was probably going to have it for dinner at some point.

I leave my bedroom and go toward the router on the stairs.

This is truly radical. Find your router. Ignore that other thing—that's where my mum's boyfriend's robot vacuum used to dock, but he took it when he left. He forgot that bit, clearly, probably a bit emotional at the time, don't look at that. Look at this. I simply put the chicken on top of the router and . . .

Totally on cue I can hear Dave running up the stairs. She spots the chicken and karate-kicks all the technology. The router tumbles to the floor and all the green lights go out. Dave drags off the chicken leg along with half of the cables.

The amount you can get done once your cat is eating the technology is incredible. It's as simple as that. If you want to get more done and eventually get to college, get a hungry feline involved. They can truly take you back to the Jurassic period, where you can do your homework in peace. And it's as simple as that! Leave any comments below and I'll see you next time. Oh, and obviously I will fix this before I try to upload. There's no need to mansplain to me. Thanks!

Erin claps for me at the end. She must have been listening all the way through. "That was seriously great, and just think how your look probably lifted it!"

"Yes," I say. "To be honest, I'm worried about Dave. She has taken some of the wireless stuff with her and I don't want her to bury it in one of her special places or take it to her panic room."

Erin looks confused. "Does Dave have her own panic room?"

"No, not really. I mean behind the couch. But it's actually really difficult to get to the back of it. Mum has to get the mop handle out to retrieve anything. And then she gets depressed because she realizes there's still stuff underneath there from when I was little. She found a *Sesame Street* domino the other day. Not even Neat Freak Gary would try to fully clean it up. Too difficult!"

I'm doing a nervous ramble speech. I know it, and I think Erin has realized, too, because she just says, "Yeahhhh," in a slightly scared way.

Then there's this huge pause. We've both run out of things that we have in common. It's the same thing that happens with the relatives you only see at Christmas. They ask you how you're doing at school and about the weather and then you just start saying anything to fill the gaps.

Erin must feel the same thing, as she decides that her mum really needs to see her about something. I thank her very much. I think she's expecting a hug, but that feels wrong so I just squeeze her arm a bit.

As she leaves she says, "I hope we can do this again, Millie. It was great working with you. I think we've taken your vlog to the next level."

I agree, though I don't know if it's the level I want to take it to. I don't like heights. I feel like we've pressed the button for the penthouse when all we really wanted was the seventh floor. Or something.

After Erin has gone, I find all the bits of machine and I manage (FEMALE POWERHOUSE!) to put the router back together. I upload the vlog while Dave plays with the chicken leg. She hasn't eaten a lot of it. I'm tempted to dust it off and put it back in the fridge, but then I remember I can't get away with that anymore. It's now on vlog record that Dave mauled the meal. Mum is off her food, anyway. She calls it the heartbreak diet. She says you're guaranteed to lose at least seven pounds in seven days but the side effect is wondering if you'll be alone forever.

If that doesn't prove that all diets are evil nothing will.

#Fool

About thirty minutes after I post the vlog, I make the very bad error of looking at the comments.

They are not good. In fact, some of them are completely horrible.

> **This is so not you. Same old. Seen it all before**
> **#unfollowed**

(This makes me feel sick.)

> **Wearing makeup makes you stupid.**
> **Parent propaganda. Do you want to force the message**
> **home a bit more?**

(I SOUNDED LIKE I WAS PREACHING! Of course I did! I could feel it.)

> **Don't mess with no date night Netflix.**

(Obviously.)

Epic makeup
I hope you realize chicken bones can kill a cat YOU
IDIOT!!

(Dave is not an average cat. I've seen her spit out fish bones in a neat pile that almost formed a sculpture. Perhaps I need to mention that.)

Is this turning into a makeup thing because if it is I'm not interested.

(No, it's not, I promise. Perhaps I should vlog about that.)

Bajka love Dave! Follow Bajka on Instagram

What?!

I open up Instagram. Bajka is a cat. She is an exotic breed with a face that looks flat like it's been squashed up. She's absolutely beautiful, though, and she writes beautifully in her own special feline language with cute spelling.

Well, obviously *she* doesn't write it. Whoever is writing for her does and it's very good. For example, there's a photo of Bajka looking annoyed. Her face is pressed up against a cupboard door.

Frenz hi. Hooman won't feed me. No tuna. Pleasz get help.

I google the name. "Bajka" is Czech for "fairy tale." This is like a fairy tale. It's the perfect account—one of the greatest Instagram feeds ever.

Bajka has got loads of followers. It's REALLY funny, too. I could never be this funny. It's like it's written by a comedian. I don't even know how to reply to a comedy cat! This is in a different league to me. It's professional and I'm . . .

I'm an amateur.

I can feel it.

I can also feel my chest getting tight and one side of me getting all tingly. This is me when my breathing gets so weird that I have to concentrate on it. Breathe in and breathe out slowly. Mindfulness, or what my mum calls common sense. God, I want my mum to come home. I look in the mirror. I still look incredible on the outside but on the inside the mascara is streaming down my face, my lips are smudged, and my entire face looks like I've flown into a patio door like a confused owl.

I lie down on my bed and slow everything up. In situations like these sometimes my brain can just shut down and I can have what I call a trauma nap. I know, I KNOW, it's not real trauma, but it's just when all the electrics in your brain feel like they are short-circuiting and you just need to put the STORE CLOSED sign up on your forehead.

Two hours later, I wake up when Dave starts biting my toe. Mum still isn't home and I'm sixty-four subscribers down.

Sixty-four. That's AWFUL. I need to speak to someone. I know I need Danny. He'll make me feel better about it all.

I send a message to him.

> Hello, Danny. How are you feeling? Are you around for a chat? Really would like to speak to you.

I can see that he has looked at my message. I wait for something back but nothing comes. This is life in the seenzone. It feels like forever. I can see he's active, but he's not typing anything to me. I get nothing.

Who is he speaking to and, more to the point, why isn't it me?!

At this point Mum comes in with Chinese takeout. She doesn't have time to put down the Singapore Noodles before I run into her for a hug. She ends up with honey and sesame dressing all over one of her best shirts, but I'm in such a state she doesn't seem to mind.

"Millie! What on earth is the matter?!" she shouts. "And why do you look about thirty-five? I'm so sorry I'm late, I was just getting this!"

"Oh, Mum!" I say, and now it's my time to get upset. I do not need any micellar water today. My tears wash off lots of Erin's brilliant work.

Mum is understanding at first, but then she does that parent thing where she suggests you should stop doing anything that might remotely upset you and that you should do something dull instead.

"I was worried this would happen, Millie. I knew it might be too much for you. It's not healthy to gauge your life success by how many random people are watching. Anyway, let me have a look at it."

I get my phone out and let Mum watch the vlog. I watch her face. She doesn't smile half as much as she normally does and occasionally she makes a tiny grimace that she tries to hide.

She draws a sharp intake of breath and gives the phone back to me.

"A couple of things, darling," she whispers gently. "For a start, you're not acting like you. You seem manic and a bit uncomfortable."

I sigh. "I know! It's all this!" I point to my face. "Lydia thought it was a good idea. I sort of hired Erin. It seemed like a good idea, but I felt all . . ."

I can't even explain it. How do you explain looking better but feeling worse?

Mum seems to understand. "You didn't feel like you. That's fine.

This isn't you right now. You'll go through lots of different versions of you before you get to the real you. In fact, I'm lots of different bits of me every day with different people. That's life. It's complicated."

This is getting a bit deep and I don't think I quite get it. Mum seems to sense this.

"Look, you're fine as you are. It's good to experiment, but at this point in a project I'd be sticking with what I know. I'd be carrying on doing what people love. And they clearly love you the way that you are. You don't have to change. This is a good thing, not a bad one!"

She's trying to make me feel better, but I don't think she understands the magnitude of what has happened. I try to explain. "But this is Lydia's specialist area. She knows what she's doing! Or she's meant to. I'm already sixty-four subscribers down!"

Mum replies almost immediately.

"Look, you've still got a ton of followers! So many that you've got representation. Millie, I won't let you do this if it makes you ill or anxious. It's not worth it. Get some perspective or get out of doing it!"

I hate this speech, but I know she has a point. I have to get tougher. I have to be more resilient. This is Granddad's favorite word. He says it all the time. He thinks millennials lack "a bit of backbone." I think he's forgotten how scary it is to be young. I don't think wondering what the hell you are doing is a new problem. I guarantee when they were building the pyramids 3,000 years ago there was someone saying, "Is a big triangle in a desert really a good idea and do I want to be part of this? I don't even get a credit on the building!"

Every human being is a little bit of a mess. Even leaders who look like they know what they are doing.

"There is another thing, Millie!"

Mum interrupts me thinking about Tutankhamun having a crisis of confidence as a teen pharaoh.

"You've just told the entire world that Gary and I have split up and that he's so emotional that he forgot part of his vacuum cleaner."

I look at her. Oh GOD, this is completely true. I was in such a weird space when I was doing the vlog I hadn't even thought. I'm exploiting my real life even when I don't realize I'm exploiting my real life.

"Mum, I'm so sorry. Do you want me to take it down?"

Mum puts her arm around me. "Too late now, love, and anyway, it's happened. I'm not ashamed of it and I don't think Gary will be watching anything we do at the moment. He's the kind of man that just cuts people off and moves on. He hasn't spoken to his brother in twenty-three years. They fell out over a plant pot. He can detach himself easily from people. He's built that way. I think he has his moon in Sagittarius. Anyway, I've spent a fortune on this takeout. Let's get eating."

I wonder what Danny's moon is in? There's no point in asking him as he thinks astrology is total nonsense. That's not his main problem, though.

The problem is Danny is *so* twentieth century. Mum always says she likes that about him. He doesn't live on his phone or through his phone. Yes, Mum, but it's not 1993 and you are not in velvet hot pants at five in the morning enjoying a sunset in REAL LIFE. Old ravers like her make out like life was good before all this. It must have been dreadful. If your friend didn't turn up, they just didn't turn up. Aliens could have abducted them and you wouldn't have found out for years, if ever!

I like to know where people are, so I like now in history. Even if that does mean that I know that Danny HAS seen my message and he's choosing not to speak to me.

I wish I didn't know that.

Mum puts the food in the microwave to reheat. Battered shrimp balls always make me feel better, even when they are a bit soggy. I'll focus on my food and try to forget about the vlog.

As Mum has also got banana fritters and ice cream, I think I'll be able to.

#Collaborator

I wake up with a brilliant full stomach and a not-so-brilliant full phone.

Lydia Portancia must have an alert for every vlog I do. She's already watched my latest vlog "a few times" and sent me this e-mail.

Hi Millie!
Watched the new one a few times now. I think it's a fantastic progression in your brand value. I sense a bit of discomfort from you, but that will pass as you get more comfortable with an everyday style of glamour. Just keep doing it. Don't worry about the lost subscribers. It's not just the numbers—it's the quality of your numbers and your audience. Better to have 5,000 subscribers with money than 50,000 with none! First rule of business!
Can you give me all the details of your makeup artist please?
Thanks Millie,
L x

Lydia is BRUTAL. She's harder than my mum. I send her a thank-you and a link to Erin's Instagram.

My agent obviously loves my new direction, but I don't—and I'm not the only one.

There is a text in capital letters from Lauren.

MILLIE. WHO DID YOUR MAKEUP? PLEASE TELL ME IT'S NOT WHO I THINK IT IS.

It IS who Lauren thinks it is, but I can't have an argument in the morning before I have toast. Carbs help confrontation. Mum is right about that.

I reply with

We'll talk at school. Love you

As I reply, Lauren walks in my bedroom door. I will have to fight this one without bread support.

"Your mum let me come up. She said you were upset!"

"I am a bit, Loz. Please go easy on me."

Lauren tries to keep her temper but can't.

"It was, though, wasn't it?"

I decide playing innocent might be a good idea.

"Was what?" I ask.

Lauren makes a face of fury. Playing innocent is not a good idea.

"You know what I mean!" she shouts. "It was Erin who did your makeup!"

"Yes, it was." I can't lie about this fact. It's obvious. "My agent thought it was a great idea and I asked her to help me."

Lauren is incredulous. "Why would you do that? Have you got amnesia? Have you had a bump to your head recently? Seriously, see a doctor!"

"Because," I reply, "she's really good at it! She gave Bradley his makeover and look how that turned out! Incredible. He looks amazing. I thought she could help me out. I don't see what the big deal is!"

I totally do see what the big deal is, obviously, but I'm trying to calm the whole situation down.

Lauren stamps her foot and starts pointing at me. She's got a very aggressive-looking finger when she's in full fury mode.

"Millie. She ruined my life and you, YOU! My best friend since forever, YOU gave her a second chance!"

I try to defend myself. "Just professionally, Lauren. It was just a business thing!"

I can't really defend it. I know that.

"Who do you think you are?" Lauren yells. "It's a betrayal of us."

"Possibly," I mutter. "But don't you think she's suffered enough? Bradley does!"

"Bradley is a lift geek. He spends most of his time looking at buttons. He's hardly a good judge of character!"

I won't have this. I don't like anyone attacking Bradley. He was bullied for years and he didn't, and doesn't, deserve any of it.

"That's not right, Loz. He's a good guy!"

Lauren starts to get a bit too harsh.

"Well, he wasn't good enough for you to go out with, so . . ."

This makes me angry. I interrupt and shout, "Can we PLEASE move on? Look, if you want the truth, I don't like the way I looked, but my agent loves it. I'm trying different ways to be viral. It hasn't worked. Give me a break. Now I've got to tell Lydia that I want to go back to NORMAL. The thought of doing that puts me in a flat-spin panic. Plus, I've lost lots of subscribers! Happy?"

Lauren sits on the end of my bed. She goes quiet.

"I'm not happy that you've lost loads of subscribers, but it does kind of serve you right. You made a deal with the makeup devil and she stole part of your soul with her evil brushes. You looked good, but you didn't look like . . ."

"Me." I finish Lauren's sentence. "I know. I KNOW! Weird, isn't it?"

And it is odd. I can't explain it. I just know that I can't ever have Erin help me again and . . .

Oh, no. I've just realized something very big and exceptionally frightening.

I sit down next to Lauren and grab hold of her hand.

"And now I have to work up the courage to tell Erin that I don't want her to do my makeup anymore. I think she thinks that she'll be doing it forever."

Lauren's eyes go wide. "Good luck with that one. I don't think Erin will take to THAT kindly at all. Even this new, improved Erin. I'll think she'll go all Incredible Hulk. Hulkess! Old Erin will be reawakened by rage."

She's probably right, too. I have to admit it.

"The thing is, Lauren, I wasn't clear. She did everything right, too. It was perfect. It was just—"

"Too Erin and not enough Millie." Lauren finishes my sentence.

Yeah, that's exactly right.

I'm still scared of Erin. I wonder if I can hide in my Zen Loo at school. I can for a while, but I can't do that forever. I'm going to bump into her at some point. She'll be looking for me, for a start. She would have read the comments on the vlog. Lots of people loved what she did. She won't be able to understand why I don't want her to help me again. Nor will Lydia.

I can't think about that. It makes me feel quite sick. Instead I think about why my best friend has appeared at the end of my bed before breakfast.

"Anyway, why are you here so early?"

"Your mum has invited my dad to have a look at your tiles."

"That was fast!" I say. I'm shocked. "She only mentioned them like, hours ago!"

"I know." Lauren yawns. "She told my dad she just wanted a fresh start as soon as possible . . . Something to keep an eye on, Millie, I think. My dad can be a bit of a flirt," Lauren snaps. "Have a look what he's doing now!"

We peek out my bedroom door. Lauren's dad is singing "Hey Jude" by the Beatles to Dave. He is using a loofah as a guitar, and Dave is purring around him like he is the best thing in the world. He is a complete cat charmer.

Lauren stares at me and pulls a face. "Yep. That happens a lot with Dad. He forgets what he is actually meant to be doing and starts playing tunes on bathroom equipment to pets. This is completely normal. Watch it, though. Some women think it's cute."

Not my mum. She would NOT fall for that sort of nonsense.

Mum comes up the stairs and starts giggling. "Oh, Rod, you are a character!" she says with a grin. Rod smiles at her and pulls a cat treat from his pocket.

"Does he always carry fish-flavored treats around with him, Lauren?"

"Oh, yes." Lauren sighs. "He prefers animals to most humans. He knows how to get them on his side."

All I can think is how easily Dave becomes friends with any random person.

"Dave will just be friends with anyone if she gets something from them!"

Lauren pulls a smug face. "Just like her owner! She's learned from the best!"

I wanted to say something really clever back, but I can't because at the moment this is a bit true.

#Link

At school it's difficult to concentrate. I'm getting stared at more than usual and the whispering around me is pretty intense. There are lots of side glances, smirks, and people putting their hands in front of their mouths. A lot of people must have noticed that I've lost followers and some people are probably enjoying it.

At lunch, Lauren comes up to me. She looks pained. This usually means she's got something to tell me that she knows I will not like.

I'm right.

"Millie. Have you had a look at your vlog?"

"No," I say. And I haven't. I daren't, really. Normally I'd be checking a lot, but I'm worried about it.

Lauren grasps her forehead. "Have a look. You need to."

Underneath one of the comments about "spectacular makeup," Erin has written:

> Thanks! I'm Erin and I do professional makeup. Find me at erinfaceforwardTM on Instagram.

"What's TM?" Lauren asks.

"Trademark. She obviously thinks she's going to end up with her own range of beauty products and she needs to kind of copyright them!"

Lauren looks outraged and yells, "UNBELIEVABLE ARROGANCE TM!"

No, it's not. It's actually forward thinking? She is thinking like an entrepreneur. Why are we bringing her down? It's genius. I wish I'd thought of that.

"Have a look at her account!" Lauren froths. "I want to see what she says!"

We look at Erin's relaunched Instagram (I'll have to send Lydia the new link).

It's amazing. She's already got lots of photos uploaded and they've got hundreds of likes. She's hashtagged to perfection and some of her looks are incredible. Day looks, night looks, fantasy looks. She doesn't put a foot wrong.

"You've got to admit it, Lauren! She is seriously talented!"

Lauren scouts through everything. I can see that's she trying to find fault, but that she can't. Lauren turns to me, holds up the phone, and points to a photo where Erin has painted glistening sea-green scales across her face.

"Yep, you are right, Mills. I don't know many sexy cod, but she's pulling it off."

This makes me giggle. "I think she's meant to be a mermaid, Lauren, but she could probably do an attractive flounder. That's the level she's at!"

At this point Lauren flings her hand across her mouth and groans, "OH, NO!"

"Oh God! What?"

Lauren puts her finger on another picture and passes me the phone.

In Erin's feed there's a selfie we did together. I didn't even think about it. I do selfies all the time. Who doesn't? I just thought Erin was being friendly. She WAS being friendly, but now I am kind of a friendly advertisement.

Lauren reads out what it says below the photo.

"It says 'This is from my latest shoot. Makeup for vlogger Millie Porter and a pat for Dave!' Then there's loads of hashtags. Like, about forty! Look!"

Lauren looks confused. "They don't do makeup for cats, do they?"

I get a bit irritated. "Of course not! She's mentioned Dave so she can legitimately hashtag #catsofinstagram and #cats on top of hashtagging all the beauty stuff. Millions of people can see it. She knows what she's doing. It's very smart."

Lauren puts her hands in the air. "Millie. You admire her! Admit it. Looks like Erin is doing your makeup forever."

"Yes, I do actually, Lauren, but she's not doing my makeup forever. She can't!" I am now completely sure about this. "It's great, but it's not right. It's—"

I don't have time to finish my sentence.

"Millie!" Erin screams excitedly. She's appeared from nowhere. "What a great reaction we've had! Have you seen it? I hope you don't mind, but I've put a link up to my new Instagram page!"

At this point Lauren decides that she has something really important to do and runs off in the opposite direction. It's just me and Erin. Face to unmade-up face.

I decide it's a good idea to compliment her but, at the same time in a very clever way, tell her that I'm going natural from now on ALL at the same time.

"No, I don't mind you linking, Erin. It makes perfect sense! And it was beautiful what you did. Like, awesome, but . . . um . . . I think I've decided to go in a different direction."

"That's exciting!" Erin exclaims. "I thought you might want to! Something a bit more dramatic. A bolder lip, perhaps? Something a bit more obvious. You can see now just how much you can get away with on-screen."

"Yeah," I mumble, "the thing is, Erin, I don't think I'm a makeup sort of vlog. You should totally do that—I'd think you'd be amazing, but I'm going to just go sort of . . . natural from now on!"

Erin stops smiling. It's like the sun has gone behind a very dark cloud. There's a pause. A horrible pregnant monster one. She stiffens up, puts her head down, and then raises it slightly. She looks genuinely upset.

She speaks slowly.

"So, can I just get this straight . . . are you telling me that you don't want me to do it again?"

I start stuttering.

"It's . . . it's . . . it's not your fault. I just didn't feel me, so I didn't act like me and—"

"I get it," Erin interrupts. "It's not what you're after? Some things are worth a try, but they don't work out."

This is awful. I could cope with nasty Erin, but upset Erin with me as the villain is the worst thing EVER.

"Please don't think of it as a dump, though. It's not a dump!" I plead. "It's a . . . reassessment of my key goals."

This is the sort of thing I hear Mum saying on the phone when she wants to stop a contract. However, from me, this does not sound convincing and Erin knows it. She looks upset but she keeps her cool.

"Seriously, it's fine, Millie," Erin says. "All the best with it. I'll keep the comment up on your vlog if you don't mind. I really enjoyed doing it for you. Thank you."

I don't have time to tell her that I don't mind as Erin leaves in a very sad way and Lauren reappears from behind some trash cans.

"Thanks for that," I bark at her sarcastically.

Lauren looks sheepish. "I didn't know what to do. What did she say?"

"She said . . . to be honest, I don't know what she said, Lauren, but basically, she's really sad about it and I caused it. I feel more Erin than Erin."

Lauren tries to make me feel better. "She's only just started this new nice Erin thing. She can't expect us to just forgive so easily! Plus, what can she do? She hasn't got the power she used to have. It's a different world now, Mills! It's all changed. She's been exposed! Don't worry about it!"

I wish I could believe Lauren, but I feel AWFUL. I hate making people feel bad. It's the same feeling when I eat too much. I get an uncomfortable feeling near my throat. Like someone is about to burst out and strangle me. That's what this feels like—internal body-based mayhem.

#Mayhem

By the time I get home, my little feeling of indigestion has turned into a full-on anxiety burp, and Mum can sense it immediately.

"What's up?"

I could try to hide things from her, but there's no point.

"I told Erin that I didn't want her to do my makeup anymore."

Mum's eyes disappear into the back of her head.

"And how did she react to that?"

"She was so upset, I thought she might cry." I sigh. "I think she thought she was doing my makeup forever and now she'll have to tell people that she's not. The thing is, I don't think I promised her anything."

"Millie! Let's get a few things straight about how the professional world works," Mum says seriously. "She re-established herself using an established brand. Classic technique. She used you. This is what happens when you're famous! You get hangers-on!"

I think it's called "support staff." She was only trying to help, but I let Mum carry on.

"It's called people who want you for what you are, not WHO you are. It's been a problem for years. Celebrities surround themselves with 'yes' people, and the next thing you know, they are releasing an album full of their dog barking. That said, I can see why she's upset."

I can, too. Surprisingly, I can easily put myself in Erin's shoes. I'd be disappointed and hurt, and inside, because of this, I'm still struggling with the fact that I might have not done the right thing. I know if I confess all this to Mum she'll be honest with me.

"Do you think I'm ungrateful, Mum?"

Mum looks at me and scratches her palm. This is a sign that she's really thinking hard about what she is saying. She's told me that she had a brain like mine. Packed full of meaty worries. I reorganize my school bag when I'm thinking and she scratches itches that don't really exist.

She puts her arm around me.

"Not ungrateful. You are ruthless, Millie. You are more sure of who you are than you think you are." Mum checks herself. "Does that make sense? Yes?"

I nod. I think I am sure of myself, but I have no idea how I feel about this fact. I will have to sleep on it.

Mum continues. "Perhaps you've got a natural business brain. That's what you need to survive. Erin offered her services. You used them, they weren't for you, and you rejected her. That's the business world. That happens EVERY day in every corner of the world."

I think Mum has forgotten I'm still in school and not an executive at an office.

Also? I think Danny has forgotten I actually exist.

#Instasham

The next day at 6:05 a.m., Lauren wakes me up with a text.

> Look at Erin's insta.

My stomach lurches.

The first photo in her feed is new. She already has hundreds of new followers. It's Erin looking atypically fabulous. Her hair is swept back off her face and her cheekbones are like knives. Not normal knives. The samurai-style ones that you see on TV that can cut through mountains and car tires.

She's not upset anymore.

She's written below the photo.

> **New day. New look. Woke up early. Thought I'd have a little play with this face? Like?**

Then she's hashtagged everything from dawn to mindfulness to cats to makeup to probably car tires.

She has LOTS of likes and her comments are incredible.

This leads to an early-morning crisis. Have I even made the right decision? Erin is a real talent. Perhaps I don't know what I'm doing.

But no, I DO. Mum is right—I am ME and I have to do what is right for me.

And you know what? I've just decided that's ALL fine because I didn't mean to hurt Erin and it's completely okay for me to have a clear sense of my own boundaries.

I know this is true.

So why do I still feel bad?

I'm so glad the school holidays start soon.

Dave saunters in and sits on the end of my bed. She shuts one eye and keeps her other big green on me. It's a power face. I need to be more like Dave. I've seen her kill cute baby squirrels in the garden. She waits till they are eating nuts on the bird feeder and then she strikes. She never shows any regret! Plus Mum is on her side because she says the squirrels are thieving off the robins and deserve everything they get.

I know where I get my ruthless streak from. Clue—it's not from my dad.

It's time to tell Lydia Portancia that I want to be natural. It's time to tell Lydia Portancia that I will decide where my vlog goes.

Not now, though. Later.

#Lesson

When I get to school, Lauren might as well have had a huge flashing sign above her head that says YOU HAVE RESTARTED THE ERIN SOCIAL MEDIA PHENOMENON! I can see that she's trying to keep it all in, but every part of her face is YELLING it.

As I approach, she sits down. I invite her to say what she likes. At times like this, you might as well get it over and done with.

But Lauren says something that I'm not expecting at all.

"I've been thinking. I have to say, Millie—and I'm being fair here to the point of giving myself a cramp—BUT I'd be hurt if I were Erin. I thought she has no feelings at all, but . . ."

I interrupt. "What was I meant to do, Lauren?! Did you expect me to just carry on with it? It wasn't right. I wasn't evil to her in any way."

Lauren cranes her neck. She tries to calm me down because she can see that I'm getting upset.

"You just dumped her. I get it, Mills. I'm just saying I'd be hurt, too. But don't worry, because GIRLS MUST KNOW GOALS!"

I know this is Lauren trying to make me feel better. Unfortunately, it doesn't help at all.

It's a reminder of another relationship that I've messed up by, perhaps, being *too* me. I'm keeping a score of them at the moment. I haven't heard anything from my dad in a few days. He has gone completely quiet. I think I've scared him off by being too emotional. I've texted him. I've left messages. NOTHING. And I don't think he's the only one, either. I look around the school. There are lots of people but someone is missing.

Danny is still not here.

I slump onto the bench next to Lauren.

"Do you know what? I don't care this morning, Lauren. Danny is not here again and he hasn't texted me and it's like . . ."

Lauren does a sharp intake of breath—"Karma! As you dump, so you shall be dumped!"

I can't have another conversation with Lauren about how karma doesn't work like this. There's no point. Secretly I really hope she's not right. I couldn't deal with it, to be honest.

Suddenly, Bradley appears. He's wearing a blazer, but it's not a school one. I think it might belong to an old airline or something. It's tailored geek from sleeve to sleeve. Let me tell you, he looks incredible. He's like a pilot who's lost his plane but seems completely relaxed about it.

"Hello, Millie," he sneers. "More drama, then?"

This is where a lot of people get Bradley wrong. He's not being nasty. He just doesn't have the same filters in his brain that other people do. Things go into his head, he shreds them like a wood chipper, and then just sprays them out at will, confetti-style. I'm usually very patient with this because I know Bradley is lovely. However, this morning I am not patient. I am very annoyed indeed.

"No, not really!" I yell. "A business arrangement didn't pan out the way we both thought it would. That's all. Nothing too serious! Anyway, who told you?"

Bradley stares at me. "Things get around. It wasn't Erin. She genuinely understands it. I've spoken to her. She's a professional. It's other people who think you've changed a bit. You do have a habit of using people and then sort of dumping them. It's sort of what you did with me."

Lauren opens her eyes wide. I jab my elbow gently into her side. I do not need for her to add to this conversation at the moment.

This is the wrong thing to say, and Bradley gets the full force of everything I'm frustrated about, from vlogging to Erin to my dad leaving and the fact I'm going to have to start vacuuming again now that Gary has gone.

"You know what, that is totally YOU bringing YOUR agenda to my day. I am NOT a user. I use people's skills and I either promote them back or—"

Lauren ignores my elbow dig and cheerfully says, "Buy them a doughnut!"

I am very grateful for this and I realize I was very wrong to try to silence her.

"Exactly, Lauren!" I nod at her and give her a small hug. "I buy them a doughnut or a coffee, so I pay for their skills. Anyway, I thought WE were friends, Bradley. This is SEXIST. If I were a boy, people would think I was just going for it in a dynamic take-no-prisoners way! Boys wouldn't be accused of dumping anyone to get what they want. It's all a huge double standard!"

Bradley looks a bit scared. "Okay! Okay!" he pleads. "I'm just saying that, perhaps—"

"Well, don't!" I shout. "I AM NOT A BAD PERSON. I AM JUST ME."

"I know that!" Bradley whispers. He backs off and slinks away, looking upset. Add Bradley to the ever-growing list of people I am mean to. I am officially *horrible*.

There's a big gap in the conversation. I shuffle my feet about a bit and Lauren scrolls through her phone. I can tell that she's not properly looking at stuff. She looks at a photo of an otter eating and doesn't favorite it. It's obvious she's not paying attention. I think she's too frightened to talk.

"That was probably a bit much, Mills!" Lauren eventually whispers.

"I know." I sigh. "I really like him, but I've just had enough. I'll apologize to him later."

Lauren gives me a big hug that I don't think I deserve and my phone vibrates. It's Mum. She does one of her legendary just-at-the-right-time psychic texts.

> Hope you're okay. Life isn't easy. Success comes with its own problems. It's not easy being a sensation. I should know.

She's joking because she adds a winky face, but Mum is a sensation in her life. I've seen people shrink in her presence, but I'm not sure I want to be that way. At the moment.

My phone goes again.

Turn notifications off, Millie! Basic error!

They're not notifications. It's another message, and it's from Danny.

> Mills, I'm a bit better. Need to c u. D x

"Oh, at last!" I exclaim. "It's Danny and he wants to see me after school!"

"That's a relief," Lauren whispers. "I thought karma was working too fast. I was thinking about all the terrible things I've done over the years!"

I am fairly sure that Lauren has not done anything too terrible as she is 87 percent wonderful, but I have to ask what.

"I'm not going to tell you," Lauren mumbles. "Just in case karma is listening. Things are okay in my life at the moment. My parents have realized they are better off not together and my best friend is going to be a vlogging millionaire so I don't have to worry too much about exams! EVER!"

This is the first time Lauren has told me about her long-term plans.

"You'll be able to buy me a house, won't you? I can just go and look after stray dogs or something . . . I KNOW! Let's open some kennels! We can call it . . . WoofHouse TM!"

I know this is silly but I would love it, so I just agree. Lauren and me working together would be peak living. There's nothing wrong with dreaming. It's actually creative visualization and all the really success-ful people in this world do it. Not just people. I think Dave does it. Next time she seems like she's just being quiet, you look at her. I think she persuaded Lauren's dad to buy her food before he came to our house. She visualized the chicken-flavored treat, and she got the chicken-flavored treat.

#Men!

By the time school is over I can't wait to see Danny. I'm ready to do a full life download. So much has happened—I need to tell him in person about my dad, my mum, all the vlog stuff, everything. I'm glad he's recovered from his terminal man flu and he's back in my zone of health and connection.

I feel a bit spoon and garbly. This is because I'm excited. I realize this doesn't make sense but, you know what it's like, love makes you a bit giddy and your toes end up somewhere near your brains.

When I get to Danny's house, I have to ring the doorbell a few times. Mrs. Trudeau eventually answers the door. She's normally firmly smart-casual (good Chanel-style jacket and perfectly fitted jeans), but today she is wearing a bright pink jogging suit. She's also modeling a very weird face. She seems a bit off. I wonder if she's just done a solid five miles or if she just been running after a solidly sick Danny. Perhaps Danny is one of these men who are really bad at being ill. She's probably had to nurse him twenty-four hours a day and bring him comfort food. To be honest, it would get on my nerves fairly fast.

"Oh, hello, Millie," she says with a bit of a grimace. "You'd better go upstairs."

"You'd better go upstairs." This does not sound good.

As I go up to Danny's room, a million things go through my head. Has Mrs. Trudeau got post-jog calf cramps? Is Danny seriously ill, or has he got a second seriously hot girlfriend he hasn't told me about? Why does the whole house feel weird? I notice that his mum has taken all the family photos down from the wall. There were lots of them in a collage. It looked fantastic. Why would she take something like that down?

Danny greets me by his door. He hugs me tightly, for a bit too long, like he is hanging on to a cliff.

"Millie—sit down," he says somberly.

I finally realize what this is about. Danny is going to finish with me because of the vlog. He's a very private guy, and he doesn't want to be part of what I've become. The partner of someone sort-of-famous. He's told his family he is going to do this, and they've moved all the pictures out of the way in case I completely lose my temper and smash them to pieces. It's so unfair! I don't deserve this treatment for being a success. I'm going to get in first.

"Look, if you're going to dump me because of the vlog then you're a sexist dinosaur. I will NOT feature you unless you want me to, and I won't talk about us EVER without your permission. I DO want to be a success, though, and that's a GOOD thing. Why wouldn't you want that for me?! I know you don't do social media and it's not 'you' and that's fine, but IT IS ME. I am a vlogger and girls will NOT be forced off the net by trolls or men who just don't get it. Also, I am not going to break anything. You thinking that is just OFFENSIVE and telling your family I'm a danger is even worse!"

This is a great speech and it covers everything I am feeling, but Danny makes a "What the HELL are you talking about Millie?!" face.

"What?! I've never accused you of smashing anything."

Now I'm confused.

"Whatever!" Danny says. "I don't care about my privacy and all that. That's not important right now. I'm sorry about your dad."

"Look," I reply, "it's all right. I'm used to it. Dad has always lived in another country. We've always found a way to talk and it's even easier now that I have my own phone. We make it work!"

Danny does one of those laughs that isn't happy—it's sort of sad.

"Yeah, I'm kind of banking on that," he mumbles.

"You don't need to bank on it," I shout. I probably *am* acting like someone who could destroy photos now. "I am telling you it's FINE. Honestly, there's only a little time difference, really, and you just keep the communication going and it's GOOD! I'm a veteran of it."

"That's what we'll do, then," Danny whispers.

"No," I have to correct him, "that's what me and Dad will do. You're just around the corner! I can see you in real life. I can pinch you!"

And I pinch him a bit too hard and have to apologize as he yelps.

"Sorry, Danny! That demonstration went wrong. The point is . . ."

What is the point? I lose my train of thought.

"The point is, can you tell me what's wrong and what the point is, because something obviously is wrong and I'm totally okay with my dad leaving!"

Danny pulls his duvet tightly around him and then takes hold of my hand. This is bad. I wonder if his gran has drowned trying to surf or something.

"Millie. We are going back to Canada at the end of this term. For good."

You know when someone's lips move and they are talking, but it's not really going in your head? That's what's happening now.

Eventually my mouth moves.

"No, my dad is going. Not you! Are you feeling okay? Is your temperature up again? Do you want me to get your mum?"

For this first time in my life, I seriously consider giving Aunty Teresa a call to ask her about medical conditions that can make you a) wear your bedding and b) act delirious. As Danny's mum was acting strange, too, it might be contagious. Perhaps they've been incubating it for months.

I sit back a bit. I don't want to catch it.

Danny gets up and starts pacing around the room. His duvet now looks like a thick superhero cape. He rubs his hands together and inhales through his teeth.

It's then I realize. This isn't raccoon virus or maple leaf fever. This is anxiety. This looks like the start of a panic attack. The moment when your head realizes it is in at the deep end, and your body starts doing things by itself you don't even realize. I, more than anyone, should have been able to recognize this.

Danny crouches down so that his face is level with mine. He looks me directly in the eye.

"No, I wasn't ill. I just couldn't face you. That's what the big family meeting was about. Leaving. I didn't know what to say. Especially after your dad announced his news."

"What?" I can't quite get this in my head. "When are you going?"

Danny pulls the duvet over his head so he is completely eaten by it. He says something, but he's muffled.

I can't believe I'm even saying this. "Danny, please come out of your blanket cave and tell me what the hell is going on."

Danny emerges and sits beside me. For the next ten minutes I get the full story. His dad came home, gathered the family together, and told them that he'd been offered a once-in-a-lifetime opportunity. It was his ultimate job. Apparently, he's had a mortal enemy in the same industry for years who always got the positions he wanted. He was always second best. This person has finally decided that she wants to travel the world for eighteen months so, whilst she's in Thailand, Danny's dad can finally get this dream gig. The problem is, it's in Toronto, and it starts in a few weeks. Each member of the family had to vote yes or no. Everyone voted yes.

"Everyone?" I ask. "Even you?"

Danny sighs. "Sorry, Millie. Yes. Even me. Dad has worked so hard, and I couldn't deny him. I knew this place was only ever going to be temporary. I just didn't know it was going to be this fast. I'm not happy about it, either."

I'm upset and outraged. In fact, I am many emotions in one handy package.

"You've only been here five minutes. Why even bother coming to school?!" I yell.

This isn't nice, but I'm having trouble taking everything in.

Danny puts the duvet over his head again. It must be his security blanket. I go close to him so I can hear him.

"This is how my life is, Millie. I'm used to dropping into schools and dropping out again. It's not this quick normally, but it is different this time. We'll stay. Dad says this one is the big one. The last one. Pension. Condo. The whole package."

I don't really care about this. The last one and the big one is in Toronto. Anything that involves a plane journey is not good news. Also, I am not used to dropping in and out. I've been around this area all of my life. I don't like change.

"But what about us?" I plead.

Danny is trying to make me feel better. "You just said it—about how you keep in contact with your dad. It's fine! We can still see each other every day. We can talk all the time. We can keep us going through THIS."

He holds up his ancient phone.

He doesn't sound convinced, and his phone does not look convincing. In fact, *this* was the phone he once lost. He retraced his steps and realized he'd put it down in the supermarket. He went back to the store, and they'd found it and locked it away in a cupboard. When the young assistant handed it to him, she said, "Aww! Bless! You've recycled your nan's old iPhone!"

It's the sort of phone you can't properly update anymore. It's not the sort of phone that can sustain a relationship.

I can't help myself—I start crying. OH GOD, WHAT IS WRONG WITH ME?! Then Danny starts crying. We are an official blub-fest.

"Mills! No, no! I've had long-distance relationships before, and I've made them work."

Strangely, this does not make me feel better.

"Hello!" I shout. "What about me? They must have ended for me to be your girlfriend! UNLESS you have a global network of women?"

This does sound ridiculous and we both smile a bit till I start crying again. I know Canada is Danny's home. I know that he wants to and needs to be with his family. It's all fair. It just SUCKS.

I need to get back in control of things. I let my anger take over a bit from my sadness. I'm sick of feeling lousy.

"I need you to know, Danny, that I've given up a lot for you."

Danny stands back a bit.

"Have you? What?" he says irritably.

This is a good question and I'm not quite sure of the answer, so I say the first thing that pops into my head.

"Important time with my cat!"

We both laugh at this and spend the next few hours chatting till Mrs. Trudeau, who is clearly very stressed, tells Danny that he needs to have a wardrobe audit as their "container doesn't have that much space." I tell Danny that I better go as, in my experience, mums go from stress to fury in under a minute.

Just as I'm leaving, Danny whispers, "Do you mind if I talk to Dave separately? We've built a relationship up and I just want to be able to talk to her without you listening."

"I think we can arrange that," I tell him. "It's important to consider her feelings."

Why am I being so sensible about this? DANNY IS GOING AWAY! FOREVER! I should be hysterical.

#Nothing Firm

I slouch home feeling completely miserable. On the way, just to make my walk a bit more interesting, I open my phone and I find another e-mail from Lydia Portancia. I know you're not meant to walk and think but I don't care.

> Hello Millie.
> I see your subscriber numbers are back up! See! This is
> what happens when you put yourself in the big league.
> You're fast becoming a really big name in this business.
> Up the production values and you up those numbers! So
> excited to see your next vlog! L x

Not so long ago, all this would have thrilled me. Right now, I feel like replying,

"Dear Lydia!
Nearly everyone I remotely care about is leaving me. No one is developing supersonic travel seriously and can I tell you what I've noticed?

Mum says troubles come in threes, but actually, men LEAVE in threes. Dad, Gary, and now Danny are all going and I DON'T CARE ABOUT MY VLOG AND I'M NEVER WEARING PROFESSIONAL MAKEUP AGAIN!"

But I am sensible and a coward so I just reply by saying, "Thanks," with three kisses. I don't like myself for this.

Mum says kisses are not professional, but I like to spread the love with random letters. Especially because I feel like I've given out too much negativity generally. Am I changing into a two-dimensional user?

It's hard to not think karma is kicking me very hard in the butt.

I flick through Instagram and realize cosmic revenge is happening.

Erin has posted an incredible photo of herself in a space-glamour pose. She's managed to make herself look as though she's falling through space with some kind of epic starry background. She's got different-colored contacts. Her eyes look otherworldly. Underneath, she's written . . .

Off the planet with happiness today. My latest look— Universe Girl TM. Delighted to announce that I'm represented by Lydia Portancia. Follow me on insta and youtube for future tutorials on getting this and other new looks XX

Erin already has nearly as many followers as me and it's compliments central with minimal trolling.

Now, I shouldn't feel jealous or angry, but I do.

At times like this I need my best friend.

I text her. I keep it factual because if I don't I will end up sobbing in the street. There's nothing wrong with crying, but my face aches from it.

I fire off the message.

Danny is going back to Canada. Permanently. And Erin is massive on Instagram and now we have the same agent.

Lauren calls me immediately.

"No!" Lauren squeals. "That's terrible. How did she manage that?!"

I think Lauren is focusing on the wrong thing here.

"By being fantastic at what she does! But that's not the crisis—Danny!!"

"Is that the end, then?" Lauren asks.

"No! We're going to have a long-distance relationship!"

"Aw! Great, Millie." Lauren sounds completely unsure. "It's just that . . . that is going to be challenging."

This hesitation annoys me. I need total confidence. *Challenging* is the word we are told to use at school instead of the words *difficult* or *impossible* or *hard*. But we ALL know it means those things.

"No, I think we can do it. Seriously, I think we can keep our passion alive!"

This sounds ridiculous, but I'm not really thinking about what I'm saying at the moment. The paper shredder in my head that eats information is stuck. Everyone has tried to put too much in it. I'm malfunctioning.

Lauren then decides to say something that is both very silly and very annoying, but only because, in the back of my brain that is going wrong, I think it might be true.

"You know what?" she says slowly. It sounds like she is burping her brains. "Your life is like a soap at the moment. Perhaps it's the curse . . . the curse of the vlog!"

What? I am regretting calling her a bit.

"I don't know—it's just weird that all this has happened to you. It's like the universe is trying to teach you something."

I can't deal with philosophy right now, Lauren.

Lauren pauses. "Just remember, Millie, the more time you spend thinking about yourself the more you will suffer. My dad said it to me. Must have been in one of those weird books he reads, as he reckons a llama said it."

Lauren means the Dalai Lama. He's not a llama. He's one of the world's wisest men. Lauren gets mixed up with things like this, but I love her for it.

There's a pause. Lauren's brain is going other planet. I can hear it over the phone. I wish I had the ability to do this. She can just fly off to other head realms and leave the lands of annoying parents and disappearing boyfriends behind.

She's on one now.

"Wouldn't it be amazing if animals did start talking and they could tell us ALL their knowledge. A guru shark! Actually, no, that doesn't work. Never go near anything that wants you for breakfast. And dinner. And a snack."

Lauren can always make me smile when I need to feel better. Eventually, she comes back to earth.

"I'm sorry, Mills. Do you want me to come over?"

I tell her no. I just want to go home, eat some chocolate, and hibernate.

"Do it!" Lauren squeals. "I'll come to yours over the weekend. My dad is coming anyway. He's doing more bathroom stuff, I think. I think your mum likes the company."

#Roaming

I drag myself into the house. Mum is home early. When I start crying, she thinks it's about Dad.

"Look, Millie, you think this is new territory, but you've been through all this before. It's fine. You'll be able to cope. Your dad was never, and never will be, the kind of man who sticks around. He has a peri . . . peri . . . peripatetic lifestyle!" Mum shouts. She's pleased with herself because she's remembered the long word she always uses for Dad. It means you never stay in one place for long. It also sounds a bit like "pathetic," which is how I feel right now.

"Mum. Danny must be peri-peri then, because he's leaving, too!"

Mum says, "Oh, darling! We aren't doing very well, are we?"

I don't really know what this "we" means, but I know that Mum calling me "darling" and being lovely to me always makes me cry even more than someone being nasty to me.

Mum gives me a huge hug. "Look, Millie! You're going to have . . ."

PLEASE no, not the men speech. The "you're going to have lots of boy-friends and you'll get your heart broken, but you'll be fine!" speech. She has a set of these—it's like a head full of TED Talks ready to go.

I let Mum finish. You can't stop her once she's started.

"That's all very well, Mum, but right now I only want one boy and he's going."

"I won't lecture you!" Mum says solemnly (too late!). "I'll just get the luxury ice cream out."

Comfort eating is sensible at a time like this. Mum and me have a spoon each, take turns, and polish it all off.

As I'm fishing out the final chocolate chip from the crease in the tub (they always hide there!), Granddad texts.

> **Your dad has got a cheap last-minute flight. Come around tomorrow to say good-bye. It's not good-bye, it's au revoir.**

My dad is leaving TOMORROW. I now know why he hasn't told me himself. He hates the thought of upsetting me. Honestly, if it were up to him, I'd think he'd just go and call me from Ibiza. I feel like telling everyone how deadly serious my life is so I do. I message back.

> **I'll be around. Dad is going, and now my boyfriend is going back to Canada, too. I think the universe is trying to tell me something.**

Granddad replies very fast for someone with rheumatism.

> **It's not the universe. It's just life. Get used to it. Now what's this flag?**

This sounds harsh, but this is Granddad. Attached to the message is an image of a flag with a smiley sun on it. I'm not in the mood for trivia, but I text back.

Argentina

Granddad is straight on it.

Being sad hasn't affected your brain. Good girl. People come and go. Knowledge is forever.

I know this is Granddad's way of trying to cheer me up, but you can't go to the prom with a fact or wearing a flag. Unless it's China. That's just red with a splat of yellow. You could pretend that little bit was a corsage.

My brain is designing dresses from flags. I need some sleep.

#Good-ByeDad

When I get to Granddad's house the next day, Dad is all packed. He doesn't have a suitcase. He has a huge shabby green duffel bag. He collects patches of where he has been. The bag is covered. He's been everywhere. The only continent he hasn't visited is Antarctica, and that's only because budget airlines don't fly there.

I have hardly been anywhere. I get anxiety going to the next city. I know he's a lot older than me, but I don't think I'll ever have the bravery to do what he's done and what he does. Not without a brain and body transplant. I can be brave on-screen but not off.

"Right, my fabulous daughter!" Dad exclaims. "Got a flight that leaves at three a.m., so I have to leave for the airport soon."

This announcement makes me burst into tears. I'm SICK of being upset. I'm tired of good-byes. My face feels like a constant puddle. This is partly sobs at Dad, and mostly still the eye miseries from Danny, to be honest.

Aunty Teresa suddenly appears with a paper bag.

"Don't worry, everyone! Millie is having a minor panic attack. Millie, sit yourself down in an upright position and breathe in and breathe out."

This does not help at all.

"I'm not having a panic attack of any size. I'm just upset!" I yell.

Granddad stares at me. "She's just having a mild attack of being a girl!"

This makes me furious, but I manage to say gently, "Granddad! People in the marines cry! It's not a female thing. It's fine. Didn't you cry when Grandma died?!"

Why does this come out of my mouth? It's true but it's a bit mean. I'm not me. Whoever me is right now. It seems to change from hour to hour.

Granddad quivers a bit and mumbles, "Yes. But dead is different than Ibiza, Millie."

I apologize immediately and try to hug Granddad, but he folds up like a cardboard box.

The whole situation gets a bit tense. Dad brings it back around to him.

"Look, Millie, you know how this works now. I'm not that far away. And there's Messenger and WhatsApp and all that. How are things going with you?"

I try to put a positive spin on things.

"Bad. No, good—well, as Granddad has probably told you, my boyfriend is leaving and I get trolls on my vlog that say evil things and upset me. But I'm finding ways to work through it."

"Here's a thing, Millie," Dad whispers like he is telling me some huge secret of life. "If someone upsets you, blank them. Ghost them. Pretend they don't exist!"

This is a stupid suggestion made by someone who still thinks it's 1995, but has learned the term "ghosting" by reading something on Reddit. I try to explain why it doesn't work that way. With Dad it's like I'm the adult.

"No. You can't shut down everything in life that hurts and sweep all your feelings under the carpet. You seem to run away from everything that might cause pain. I'm not being Dr. Phil, but why don't you just face up to the fact you are going away and we are going to miss each other and that HURTS. DEAL WITH THE REALITY!"

Dad tilts his head down and looks a bit shamefaced.

"Yes!" Teresa yells. "You HAVE to face up to your DEEP emotions, deal with them, and move on. This is why I looked up Marie Castellanos on Facebook! She made my life hell at school. I found her profile photo and shouted at it and then I moved on. I was cleansed of her bad energy and my past pain. She's a dental nurse now. I bet she loves seeing people in agony! She's just got back from Florida."

"How do you know?" I ask.

Teresa pulls a face. "Obviously, I've had to look her up regularly to check she's not after me."

"Why would you torture yourself?" Dad says wearily. "I haven't got enough time for the people I love, let alone the people I can't stand. If people upset me, I just cut them out. Try it."

Teresa and me look at each other and pull identical "He doesn't really get it, does he?" faces. I've tried to explain. Sometimes you have to accept you can't change people. In fact, all the time.

Dad looks at his watch. He's one of the few people I know who tells the time with something on his wrist and not on his phone.

"Right, Millie, I've really got to go. I've got to get the bus to the airport seven hours early just in case of traffic."

I hug Dad tightly. I'm already sick of good-byes. They make me sad. And I've got more to come. I take a photo of Dad's bag and stick it on Instagram with this description.

Won't be vlogging for a few days. My dad is going to live abroad again and I'm feeling a bit over it.

I can't tell people about Danny yet. I just can't face it. That's for a time when I'm feeling a bit stronger. I don't want everyone to see me crying. I am NOT a good crier. My face collapses.

On the way back to my house Granddad sends me a text with another flag.

Millie, this is Guatemala.

It has a lovely bird on it and guns.

Hope you're okay.

I love Granddad even when he's weird. He'll never move abroad. Mainly because with his hip he can't actually walk that far.

Once I get home, I go upstairs and realize that Rod, Lauren's dad, is there working on the mortarboard. My mum is directing him like he's someone she manages at work. Really, my mum bosses everyone around. I like that about her, though, and I like the fact that it's just us again.

"Ah! Millie!" She looks really happy to see me and gives me a huge hug. Rod smiles and sings another song to Dave, who is perched near the shower head listening to every word.

"Isn't Lauren with you?" I ask.

"Nah," Rod says quietly. "She wanted some time with her mum. They are doing girl stuff. You know."

"What IS girl stuff?" Mum asks him angrily.

Rod smiles. "Anything females want to do. Motocross. Heavy lifting. Clothes. Protesting. Designing bathrooms. Women can do what they like."

Mum laughs at this and Rod grins at her and winks. Mum and Dave love Rod. They haven't seen his temper like I have. I have seen his darker side. It's not all silly songs and skills. He's made my best friend's life very tough at times. I'm a bit wary.

"Do you know what? What a great idea!" Mum says enthusiastically. "I thought we'd go to look at tiles this weekend. We can create our new bathroom together!"

I know Mum is trying to be kind, but I don't think this is a good idea. She's trying to take my mind off Danny and my dad with tiling but, yeah, my mum is trying to take my mind off some of the most emotional stuff in my life by going to the shop for little ceramic squares.

It doesn't sound like the world's most successful plan, but anything is better than sitting in my bedroom for too long thinking about my life and how it's turning very odd karma corners.

#Duffel

As soon as I wake up, I check my Instagram. There's been a huge reaction to the photo of my dad's bag. It's only when I look at it for the first time in a while that I realize how cool it looks in a Hudson filter.

There arc lots of comments.

> **OMG! Has your dad been to Chile? I have always wanted to go there! It sounds incredible!**

(I've always wanted to go, too. I love the way it's very long but looks about three miles wide.)

> **Totally understand your feelings.**

(Thank you, RainbowGirlUnicornFeelings!)

> **Stop going on about your dad. Mine left when I was 3. I haven't seen him since.**

(Why do people follow me if I get on their nerves?!)

I wish my dad would leave. That would be good.

(This is a reply to the comment above.)

What a really cruel thing to say.

(Now they are arguing.)

You have no idea of my family!

(No, we don't. How could we?)

And you have no idea of mine.

Where is this even going? Why are two people having an argument on my Instagram page?! It's a PHOTO OF A GREEN DUFFEL BAG WITH PATCHES ON IT.

I lose forty-seven followers, but I pick up fifty-two.

If people don't want me warts and all, then I don't want them. This is absolutely what I should be thinking. I should be ignoring them and focusing, as Lydia Portancia would say, on my brand. It makes perfect sense.

Of course, instead of doing this I look at all their profiles and try to work out why they don't like me anymore. I also still haven't told Lydia that my next vlog will be *au naturel*, makeup-free Millie.

Jump that fence, Millie, when you need to, the implanted Mum in my brain says.

Right at the bottom of my post I see the comment.

Bajka, the brilliantly funny cat, has sent me a comment and a heart.

I should feel happy about this but I just feel jealous that a cat says all the right things when I mainly say the wrong ones.

Also, Erin appears on a sponsored post in my timeline. In summary, she is a diva now promoting a lip gloss and I am a vlog about random bits of my life and a cat.

For the rest of the morning, I am mainly very bored indeed in a home interior warehouse. The trouble is, Mum and I cannot agree on something we both like. I like bright and patterned. Mum likes white. Just white—not even white with a nice patterned trim.

* * *

Here are the things I learn from walking miles and miles around bathroom showrooms:

1. Tiles are dull.
2. Bathroom suites can cause huge arguments between couples. I think I witness a divorce starting today over a soap dish.
3. Tiles can cause huge arguments between mothers and daughters.
4. Your boyfriend who is JUST ABOUT TO LEAVE will text you whilst your mum is looking at sinks, and your mum will say, "MILLIE! CONCENTRATE!" like FAUCETS MATTER. Who cares what a faucet looks like as long as water comes out of it?!

Mills, we are busy packing and clothes auditing but want to see you lots. Can you come around this afternoon?

"Can I go and see Danny?" I plead with Mum. "I think you have a very clear vision of what water dispensers you would like."

Mum looks at me with exasperation.

"Yes, fine!" she blurts. "BUT I do like the simple look, and I have an aesthetic power veto!"

I just nod. If Mum wants the world's dullest bathroom, she can have it. I hope she and Rod finish it soon, though. He has a tendency to sing classic albums while he is working. The other day he re-enacted something called "Dark Side of the Moon" by Pink Floyd by hammering nails into floorboards and wailing at the top of his voice. I don't mind, but Dave hovers around him like a major fangirl and tries to join in. She really is shameless.

#Huevos

As I'm walking to Danny's, I put some music on. Walking with my music normally clears my head—even a head full of strangers and clever or disloyal cats.

Today, though, things are different. I see Bradley with someone new and furry.

Bradley is walking a new dog.

This is quite a shock. I don't quite know why, but I feel like if Bradley has a new pet he should tell me. It's a pretty big deal. This is a new woman or man in his life—I should be informed! This is of course ridiculous—it might not even be his dog.

Bradley strides toward me with massive, lanky man-steps. He looks very excited to see me. His new pooch seems a bit more nervous.

"Millie!" he exclaims very loudly for him. "I'm so glad to see you!"

I crouch down and stroke the new dog.

"And who's this then?" I think I probably sound a bit annoyed.

"This is Huevos. Huevos is a Staffordshire-Chihuahua cross. He's great, if I do say so myself."

Huevos licks me. He's very friendly.

"Where did you get him from?"

"From the shelter," Bradley whispers. "We don't like to talk about it. He hasn't had the best start. To be honest, I don't like his name but it's too late to change it. I wanted to call him Otis after my favorite elevator company but Huevos didn't recognize it."

Huevos sits down and starts to wash himself. It seems a bit of a weird thing for a dog to do in the middle of the street.

"Oh! Yeah. Another thing." Bradley grimaces. "He also thinks he's a cat."

This makes me giggle a lot. Bradley gets a bit annoyed and defensive.

"He thinks he's a cat," Bradley explains. "It's because he spent most of his early life with an old woman who had seven of them. She just fancied getting a small dog and, understandably, THIS small dog thought he was like everyone else in the room. Sometimes he tries to purr. Of course, it's other dogs we have a problem with. He's a cat. He hates them! He tries to attack them. We are thinking about going to an animal psychologist."

I try not to smile but it's very hard.

Suddenly, Huevos sees a Labrador on the other side of the road and starts rolling on the ground. He barks and lunges and snarls. The owner of the Labrador looks very unimpressed. Bradley shouts, "Sorry! He's got issues!"

This makes me laugh and I feel a bit better. Huevos is a lovely furry distraction.

Bradley winks at me. He realizes that this is a little bit funny.

"He likes lifts, though. I might start featuring him on my vlog. I'll pretend he's an assistance dog. That way we can go everywhere together. I do think he understands me more than most humans do."

I can believe this. Bradley looks really handsome these days but most people still think he's a bit weird. It's their loss. I love being with him, even when he does have a snarky moment.

"He's going then," Bradley blurts out on cue. "Your man is leaving us."

Correction. I *did* love being with Bradley. This annoys me. The Danny news has gotten around quick!

I look down to the ground and shuffle my feet.

"I haven't even announced it yet!" I say crossly.

"It's not really your news to announce, though, is it, Millie? Danny is telling people." Of course, this is correct, but I don't like the thought of people knowing the truth. It makes it more real.

Bradley can see I'm upset.

"Shame," he says with a shrug. "I thought Danny was a good guy."

This is an out-and-out lie, and I'm not having it. "You hated him!" I shriek. "You never liked him—and less of the past tense, please! He IS a good guy!"

"I didn't hate him." Bradley is very defensive. "I don't hate anyone, Millie, and I know you liked him!" Bradley corrects himself. "LIKE him!" Bradley looks down. "I've had long-distance stuff, and I know it can hurt."

I forget that in the world of lifts and elevators, Bradley has a global-geek thing going on. He's done long-distance relationships before.

I ask him a question that I just want the answer YES to.

"Can you make things work?"

Bradley sighs. "It's not easy, but it's possible."

I just wanted him to say YES, but Bradley will give you the truth. He's not capable of giving anyone anything else.

"How do you make it work?"

Bradley crouches down to Huevos and starts to stroke him. "Keep all lines of communication open. Message each other, see each other, be prepared to be awake at funny times of day to be there for each other, don't forget what brought you together in the first place and—"

Huevos starts wrestling with his leash. He's spotted a Doberman headed our way and he wants a fight with it.

"Huevosssssssssssss!" Bradley semi-yells. "Sorry, Millie, I need to go."

"Can I talk about your relationship on my vlog, Bradley?"

Bradley shouts as he's being pulled down the street. "Yeah, if you want. Don't mention Huevos yet, though, yeah? I'm a bit embarrassed, as he's technically a problem dog."

Bradley disappears with Huevos yapping like a crazy thing. I always feel better after seeing Bradley. He's sensible like I'm sensible. We fit together, really.

Not in that way, though. It's Danny and me forever, before you get any ideas.

When I get to Danny's house, it's already half packed up.
It's wall-to-wall boxes. The Trudeaus have made little pathways through them all so you can get to different rooms. It's like being in a subway system. Danny can see I look a bit horrified.

"It looks bad," Danny says, "but we didn't bring too much with us in the first place. We knew we wouldn't be around forever. Most of my stuff is in storage. There's not a lot of need for ice hockey equipment in this city."

"Ice hockey. I never knew you did that!" Who is this man that I call my boyfriend?

"Oh yeah, I LOVE it!" Danny's eyes are like saucers. You can tell this is something that he ADORES. "You know there's a machine called a Zamboni that smooths the surface of the ice. You can drive it! It shaves the ice like a razor on skin, then it smooths it all inside. THEN it spews it out to make recycled ice that you can skate on!"

"Wow," I reply with an unwow voice. I realize that Danny comes from another world. A world of snow.

We spend the rest of the afternoon together. It's like it always is—he's funny and he's sweet. He does an incredible impression of not just a Zamboni but a moose, the teacher at school who gets a bulgy vein forehead thing when he gets cross, and a pedestrian crossing. Don't ask how. He just does.

It's all going fantastically until he starts to talk about leaving, and then he gets serious.

"Can you do me a favor after I'm not here, Millie?"

"Depends what it is," I say cautiously. Mum says never go into negotiations blind. You have to know what you're doing.

Danny looks fidgety.

"Stop worrying so much. HAVE FUN. Have fun in this space and place right now. Because I've moved around so much, I've discovered that. If you aren't where you are, you're nowhere. I didn't think of that—I saw it on TV—but it's TRUE. And ignore the trolls. They are nothing to you. They are THIS!"

Danny starts to do an impression of a fly that buzzes around me for a time, then dies horribly in the middle of the floor. His legs go everywhere.

"They are THIS!" Danny shouts to me again. "And you are Millie Porter. You've got this incredible thing going on. Don't ruin it!"

It's hard to take advice from someone pretending to be an insect, but I know he's trying to be kind. And I know he's right.

When I go to leave, we have a tremendous kiss. It reminds me exactly of what I am going to miss. It goes on forever till his mum shouts up to say that his dinner is ready. Mums seem to have a sixth sense when it comes to anything even slightly passionate. One bit of tongue action and all of a sudden the pasta is boiled and will self-destruct if you don't come and get it immediately. It must be something they teach you in parent school.

When I leave, Danny hugs me very tightly. The kind of hug you can still feel in your skin after the person has gone. The best kind. Not too tight, but real and firm. Danny is leaving, but he doesn't have to leave my head.

The whole afternoon has made me feel a bit braver. I think I'm ready to share my news with the world now. I think I'm ready to admit that . . .

Danny is going.

There. I managed to say it without losing the plot.

As I'm walking home, I get a message from Dad. Sometimes he texts things he wants to say, but can't.

> Millie. I love you and I think what you are doing is marvelous. You've inspired me. BTW my plane is late. Pilot strike.

I'd prefer not to be an inspiration and for people to stick around. That would be good.

#LongDistanceVlog

As I get home, I have repeated the mantra "Danny is going" many times without folding into a miserable heap of blubs, and I am ready to vlog.

I sit myself in front of my desk in my room and set everything up. Normally, as soon as I get in, Dave would be trying to get some food off me, but she's nowhere to be seen. I check in her panic room, behind the bookcase, and under my bed. I finally find her in the bathroom. Rod isn't there, but Dave still looks like she's waiting for him. I think Dave has a cat crush on Rod. She's pining for him and his singing. When I pick her up, she tries to jump back into the empty bathtub. I have to coax her out with lots of strokes and a tickle between the ears. I also promise her some blue cheese and ham. We don't have either, but one thing Dave cannot yet do is check the fridge on her own. This is sort of lying to her, but sometimes, when you're vlogging, you have to do it. I carry her downstairs, collect some cereal boxes from the kitchen, and give her a standard mini fish cat treat. Dave is unimpressed.

When we are back in my room, I put Dave on my lap and press RECORD. I'm bare-faced and "me," and Lydia is just going to have to deal with it.

Hi, everyone. I've got some huge news for you.

Hashtag Help my boyfriend is leaving and he's going back
to his home of Canada! Now, I think we can totally make it
work. You tell me, though—can we? The main problem with
Canada is this . . .

I get my children's atlas out. It's a bit embarrassing as it has a cute
cartoon whale explaining facts about all the different oceans but it's the
only one I've got.

. . . look at Canada. It's big. It's huge. And it's not near
where I live. A massive amount of land mass full of fantastic
wildlife like beavers.

Beavers are incredible. Say, if Dave were a beaver . . .

I start to put cereal boxes around Dave until she is completely
surrounded.

. . . she would build her own dam. And there she would
sleep, eat, and raise her young.

Dave looks horrified at this farce and show jumps out of the cereal-
box dam without knocking a box over.

But, as you can see, Dave is not a beaver and I am not
Canadian.

I'm asking you, really. Can this work? My friend Bradley had a long-distance relationship with a lift expert and um, yeah, he thinks it can.

Dave comes and sits directly in front of the phone.

Dave also wants to know, as you can see. Happy owner. Happy pet. She's a bit sick of seeing me upset.

At this point, Dave decides she's going to flop onto my cheek.

I know loads of you maybe feel the same way. I'm sorry things have been a bit heavy lately, but life has just felt really intense. Lots of things have changed, and—

Dave moves in front of my mouth. To avoid the risk of getting a furball, I stop talking for a moment until I can gently move her out of the way.

Dave has spoken and the people have spoken. Please leave a comment and subscribe, and we'll talk again soon.

I look at Dave. "There's no need to be quite so rude," I tell her. Dave just shrugs and goes back to the bathroom. She goes and sits by the washing basket. My cat is in love with another human and I need to face that fact and upload another video. I am not going to check for comments in the middle of the night, either. This is a new, balanced Millie. I am going to practice mindfulness and fall asleep with thoughts of being a jet-set teen who can fly and see her boyfriend whenever she feels like it. I can hire a private tutor and do my high school exams in the first-class cabin. I have grown a bit of a Lauren lobe in my brain. It's very unrealistic, but very comforting.

The next morning, I surprise myself by waking up at 6:25 a.m. and not at 2:36 a.m., when the desire to check for comments is at its very strongest. I even manage to brush my teeth first before I pick up my phone.

When I get to the bathroom Dave is still in there and has moved inside the washing basket. She is wearing a pair of my dirty jeans as a scarf and looks a bit sad. I think she misses riding the robot vacuum. Sometimes I find her looking longingly at the docking station. Toward the end of Mum and Gary, she used to lie down and let the vacuum go around and de-fur her. Change is hard for cats. And humans.

Finally, once I've fed Dave, I look at the comments that people have left. There are times when being a vlogger is great. Today is not going to be one of those days.

Cheat potential is massive

(Thank you for stating my worst fears.)

Face it. To him you were a holiday fling.

(This is not a holiday.)

You can't commute to Toronto.

(Why do people state the obvious?)

Dave is JOY. Give Dave to me.

(No. She's lovely and she's mine.)

It's OVER. No Way Jose.

(I wish I hadn't looked at it now. And who is Jose?)

My dad he a lorry driver. He loves my mum

Basically, long-distance relationships are doomed unless you're a trucker. I'm beginning to think that all relationships are doomed, but I've picked up loads of followers. Perhaps people like bare-faced bad news.

I've also picked up a new e-mail from Lydia.

> Millie,
> Powerful new vlog. Sorry to hear about your news. Think
> the bare face suited the naked emotions. Thinking though
> this is a one-off natural look? Is that right? I represent Erin
> Breeler now. Thank you so much for introducing me to her. I
> think she'll continue to focus your brand.
> L

L with no kiss. Noted.

I am very tempted to go back to bed at this moment but I decide to go visit Aunty Teresa and Granddad. They will be missing Dad. Probably even more than me. I'm doing a Dalai Lama and thinking-of-others thing to ease my suffering.

I also have three pieces of toast before I go because, you know, the cheer-up power of carbs. There's no meat on it, so it's completely Buddhist.

Honestly, I could also do with the company and some advice. Perhaps I have gotten a bit too heavy and serious—the opposite of heavy and serious is Teresa.

#Bats

When I get to Granddad's house, I let myself in. The house is very quiet. I look around. It's sad without Dad. It's like a balloon with most of the air let out of it. I can hear someone moving upstairs and I can tell it's Teresa because she clomps her feet like a horse. I don't tell her I'm in the room. I just fancy a moment to get used to all this and the new situation.

When Teresa finally does come in the living room, she doesn't say, "Hello," she greets me by saying, "Millie. Promise me one thing: You'll never pick up a bat! You can never be too careful."

Even Teresa has had a slight attack of the sensibles these days. She's learning about tropical diseases and sometimes comes out with the most random pieces of advice ever.

I don't want to ask, but I have to. "Why?"

Teresa looks at me like I should know and the answer is obvious.

"Bats are just a flapping nocturnal mound of terrible death!" Teresa shrieks. "Rabies. Lyssavirus. For all we know, vampire . . . disease!"

I find knowing about illnesses just leads to more worry, so I try to escape from Teresa fast. She isn't that easy to get away from, though, when she's in this mood. She wants to tell you everything she knows.

"Possums, though," she continues, "they are mainly fine. Very clean animals with cute faces. Just don't corner them in a store. They can turn very nasty if you threaten them in the chilled food section. Have a look on YouTube! How's the vlog going, anyway?"

It's very hard to keep up with Aunty Teresa when she's like this but yes, THE VLOG. I'm worried I'm boring people like Mum and Lauren. Perhaps Teresa can give me a new opinion on things.

"It's hard," I tell her. "I've got to keep my profile up, but producing interesting stuff all the time is hard."

Teresa nods at me. "Yeah, because you need things to go viral a lot. It's become kind of serious. It's all very (*and she does an impression of me*) 'I'm going to miss my boyfriend.' I think you need to remember your core audience a bit more."

This is very annoying, and I wish I hadn't asked.

"Thanks for that, Teresa!" I reply grumpily. "Do you vlog often?"

"No, BUT I watch lots of them. A lot of my medical knowledge comes from experts on the net!" she says proudly. "I could take an appendix out with a coat hanger. Probably. If it was an emergency on a plane."

I can't think that's a good thing. I'm too angry right now.

"People follow you for fun, Millie. You need to get something out there that's just a bit fun and light and frothy!"

I know Teresa is right, but I just don't feel this way at the moment. So, I snap at her and feel bad immediately afterward.

"I'll tell you what—when you're a viral sensation you can tell me how you managed it!"

Teresa manages to remain really calm. "You're very irritable, Millie. Have you had your hormones checked recently for imbalances?"

I find my inner sass. That, at least, has not left me.

"No. But I have been checked for annoying aunties and I've got a positive result!"

Teresa, at this point, would normally storm out of the room, but she has a new air of authority. She sits on a dining room chair and leans forward like she is a doctor doing a consultation.

"Millie, I am going to choose to ignore that, and I'm going to think of a way to put fun back into your life. It's part of my remit as a health-care professional and as your aunty."

I'm a bit suspicious of Teresa's attempts at positivity, but I haven't got the energy to argue. I want to see Granddad. At some points in your life, you just need old.

#Seeds

I find Granddad in the place he loves the most: his shed.
He has made it a potting paradise again. It's almost like I never ever
vlogged here. There's a few fairy lights left over a shelf. Granddad is
staring at a tiny sapling. I think he might be talking to it, as I hear him
whispering, but he stops when I come in.

"Hello, Millie," he says with his beautiful crinkly grin. "I was just
telling this thing it's doing a good job growing. People might think I'm
nuts, but if it's not hurting you and it's not hurting anyone else, I say you
can do as you like."

I stand beside him and put my arm on his shoulder.

"Granddad—everyone is going!" I moan.

Granddad gives me a tiny hug. It's a strong one, though.

"I bet it feels that way, Millie, but let me give you a very important piece of advice. What's for you won't go by you. You haven't had
a disaster. You've had life, Millie. People come and go. And they find a
way to stay, too. Sometimes whether you like it or not. When your gran
died, she told me to water the plants in the kitchen. They were plastic.
She knew what she was doing. There's a way to stay in someone's life

even when you're not around. You're going to have lots of loss. I won't be here forever."

I wish old people wouldn't go on about death so much. It really makes me feel sick.

"If people are here"—he points to his heart and thumps it—"then that's where they are, and that's where they stay. And that's as soppy as I get, my girl, so go and do some of that thing you do. Teresa showed me. You're good at it."

I love my granddad. My relationship with him is so pure and lovely, even when he is a sexist dinosaur. My relationship with my dad is weirder. He comes and he goes, but he's in my heart and he'll never leave. It feels the same way with Mum and Dave.

Can I be honest? I don't think it's going to be the same with Danny. Do we really get each other?

Maybe I'm expecting too much. There's no perfect match in the world—that doesn't exist. *Shut up, Millie.* He's handsome, he's funny, he's different. He's still going.

I check my vlog again. I have lots of views now.

Why do so many women want to settle down? There's more to life than relationships. Education! Travel! PETS. Dave your cat is incredible. Focus on him.

EscapadeDreams is clearly my mum. She's pretended she doesn't know Dave is a "she" to make it look more realistic. How many profiles can one woman have?!

She's right, though. I won't tell her that, but she is.

177

#FarewellFortnight

Over the next two weeks, Danny and I spend a ton of time together. I'm hardly home. Mum is busy working out stuff with Handyman Rod. The bathroom ends up looking incredible. Perhaps blue and yellow twists (my idea) was too brave. Lauren keeps messaging me asking me if her dad is with my mum with an eye roll emoji, but I haven't been worried about that too much. It's all about Danny right now.

We go to the movies, we hang out in his room, we hang out at my house. I don't do any crying and I'm a nonstop comedy machine. The truth is, I don't want to turn into a girl who waits.

But Danny has a lot of good-byes to do, so I DO turn into a girl who waits. And just before he's due to go, he drops a bombshell. He doesn't want me to come to the airport, as he thinks they are very charged places. I had absolutely banked on seeing him and his family off at the international terminal. I had the scene in my head! I knew how it was going to pan out, and what we were going to say to each other.

Finally, the moment comes when the suitcases are packed, Danny's mum has checked the passports about fifty times, and the Uber driver is waiting, looking at his phone and getting more annoyed. The house is cleared and locked up, so there's no alternative.

Danny and I say good-bye near a Dumpster.

Not any old Dumpster, either. A Dumpster that people are taking things from. It's hard to be romantic when someone is wondering whether Danny's parents have thrown out a priceless antique. CLUE—the label says Ikea. I don't think they were around in the eighteenth century.

Danny and I have a final huge hug. He starts tearing up, but manages to keep it in. That's what toxic masculinity does to even lovely guys. It makes them scared just to lose it in the street. I tell him he can cry. It's the sign of a real man.

Danny looks at me tenderly. "Millie. I think I need to be strong for both of us."

"No, really, you can cry," I reassure him.

"I'm okay, Millie," Danny says.

If this weren't our good-bye, I'd let myself be a bit annoyed at this. He doesn't have to be strong for both of us. I can handle my feelings, thank you. Also, he's frankly not as upset as I think he should be. Sometimes being so laid-back and "Zan" seems a bit inappropriate. I'm quite grateful for the anger, as it stops me going into full snotty-mess mode.

Danny finally gets in the car. As it pulls out of the driveway, he waves and blows me a kiss.

I discover an important fact—sidewalks are lonely, and empty houses are huge, sad, hollow reminders of people who are just about to fly thousands of miles away from you.

I text Lauren. **He's gone.**

Lauren texts back with

Don't forget, just like me, he's just a text away. We all live on earth! And earth is tiny compared to Jupiter.

179

There's no intelligent life on Jupiter, I message back.

There isn't much at school but we cope, Lauren snaps back.

By the way have you ever seen a camel's mouth? Google it.

I do, and I wish I hadn't.

It does take my mind off Danny, though.

When I get home, I check my e-mails. I'm not as upset as I'd thought I'd be about Danny, to be honest. Or I'm not until I read the latest e-mail from Lydia Portancia.

> Hello Millie! Where's a vlog? Let's keep that heat up on your brand! It bonds that relationship with the audience. It's the daily stuff that keeps us connected with you as a REAL person. People get bored very fast. Keep it personal, keep it you, and keep it coming at us! Has the boyfriend gone? How does that feel?
>
> L

I'm not a brand. Lydia treats me like Coca-Cola—not a human being. I am not brown fizzy water. I have feelings. There are times when the only logical and very sensible thing to do is to go to bed very early. I put Lydia Portancia away in the compartment of my brain marked "Later" and close the curtains. Good night, world. For the rest of the day, all of humanity is officially canceled.

#TransportGuru

The next morning, I wake up with nothing to do and Lydia Portancia's e-mail hanging over me. I don't feel like being happy or pretending everything is okay. It's not. But I don't want to do another Debbie Downer vlog either. I'm lying in bed trying to read *Jane Eyre* AGAIN when Bradley FaceTimes me.

He doesn't bother saying hello. He comes straight out with the geek.

"Do you know who Danny is flying with? I can track his flight on my app for you if you like. Air traffic is incredible. There are queues of planes."

"How does that even work?!" I reply. "How do they keep everything in the air without things bumping into each other? COULD DANNY'S PLANE BASH INTO ANOTHER ONE?!"

Bradley looks at me. He can see he's given me a worry seed that's growing in my mind.

"He'll be fine, Millie! The chance of a midair collision is very low. As long as the TCAS works. It's a collision system. Always listen to TCAS, Millie, and not to the air traffic controller."

I tell him that if I ever do become a pilot I will keep that in mind. Bradley will turn almost every conversation to escalators or transportation. They are his happy places.

"How are you feeling, anyway?" Bradley says. He sort of barks the question, but I know he cares and I know he means it.

I tut. "You know. Okay. Fed up. My agent woman isn't helping."

"You're big, Millie. She knows that. You've got to keep that up."

How to explain it? I'm sick of sharing my emotions and blurting my brain everywhere. Before all this started, I used to go and hide in my Zen Loo or my bedroom when I had a crisis. Now, I feel sometimes like there is nowhere to hide. I can't tell Mum this. She'd just say, "I knew all this was too much for you. Stop vlogging. Take it all off. Delete your account!" So, I say nothing. I keep it all in.

I don't tell Bradley all this, either. I just say, "I don't feel like it."

This sounds lame, but it's all I can manage.

"I think you need to remind yourself of why you started doing this in the first place," he says with a smile. "I have an idea. Can you bring Dave around to my house?"

"Yeah, I suppose," I say. "Why?"

"I've got an idea. It might work. If it doesn't, it doesn't matter, and if it does, then . . . that's good."

This is Bradley's beautiful way of trying to cheer me up. It's appreciated. I tell him I'll be around as soon as I get dressed.

#DynamicDuo

I explain to Dave that I need to put her in her cat carrier.
This gives her the fear, as normally this means she's going to the vet for a shot. Dave does not like the vet. Things have happened at the vet that can never be spoken of. I manage to tempt her in with part of my toast and walk around to Bradley's house. She moans all the way there and only stops when Bradley makes a fuss of her. He is one of the few people on earth who is allowed to stroke her ears.

"What have you got in mind?" I ask Bradley.

He has his maximum-strength glasses on. His eyes look huge. The frames really suit him, though.

"What I have in mind," Bradley announces proudly, "is Huevos!"

At the mention of his name, Huevos comes in and looks at Dave's pet carrier with total fear.

"Don't worry, Huevos!" Bradley reassures him. "You're not going back to the shelter. This is someone new for you—Dave!"

"Is this safe?" I ask.

"Of course it is!" Bradley tells me. "Huevos thinks he's a cat. I thought what we could do is introduce them on film and link it in to you meeting new people because, you know, people have left your life and now you have to, perhaps, think about new people."

Bradley can see I'm going to explode at this, so he adds quickly, "—WHILST still speaking to the old people in your life and maintaining your relationships with them. It's cats. It's dogs. It's friendships. I think it could work really well."

I realize Bradley may be on to something here. Perhaps I can do something that's funny, but still me and about my life.

"Have a little think!" Bradley says. "You can vlog in my room. It's set up for it. I occasionally do stuff from there when I'm not mobile and exploring lift systems. I don't want to be in this, though. I'm not really comfortable with it."

This astounds me. "But you vlog all the time. You've got a huge following, Bradley!"

Bradley is firm. "I vlog on my specialist subjects. I don't vlog feelings. That's not my brand. My arm can be featured and my name, but that's it."

I don't need to think. This is a great thing to do. It's certainly better than any vlog ideas I've got. I don't want to cry about Danny. I tell Bradley we are on. First, he takes Huevos out of his room so we can get a dramatic entrance. Then he holds my phone and presses RECORD.

> Hello! Sorry I haven't been around for a while. As lots of you know, I've had a lot going on. It's sort of a new chapter in my life and Hashtag Help I need to make new friends. It's a very common problem. I've had a lot of change and I get that other people may be in the same boat. The thing is, I often look for people like me, but friends can be lurking in the weirdest places.

I'm at my friend Bradley's house with Dave. Bradley
is really into lifts. You may have heard of his vlog, The
King of Elevation. I am not into any of that, BUT Bradley
and I are good friends. Good friends can be kind of
unexpected.

Dave is here to meet Huevos, Bradley's dog.

I let Dave out of the carrier. She gets out very nervously, and Bradley
lets Huevos into the room.

Huevos approaches Dave, and then he and Dave start nuzzling like
they've known each other for years.

This is Huevos. He thinks he's a cat, and as you can see,
this is love at first sight. Sometimes that's the thing. Finding
new friends and your tribe can mean hanging around with
people very different from you. Perhaps there are people
who think very differently, like Huevos, but that doesn't
make them not fantastic to be with.

At this point Huevos's wagging tail accidentally whacks Dave in the
face. Dave would normally have a complete feline tantrum at this, but
she just purrs her face off.

It's an incredible scene.

Anyway, that's it. I'm going to be like Dave and Huevos and
just think out of the friendship box a bit more. Lauren, don't
worry, you're my best friend and I still love you. AND YOU,

Dave, obviously. Some people are irreplaceable beings of wonder.

Dave ignores me. Only Huevos exists for her right now.

Thank you for all your lovely comments, please subscribe, and dogs and cats forever.

This makes Bradley laugh out loud. He's not a huge fan of humor, so this feels like a bit of an achievement. I think I will keep that in the final edit.

"See!" Bradley says. "That was really good. And Dave and Huevos were fantastic. It had a serious point to it, too, but it wasn't pathetic, like—"

I know Bradley wants to say, "Like your vlogs have been," but he saves himself and says, "—people who do those vlogs that are all emotions and tears and stuff."

I can't get cross at Bradley. I have been a bit soft recently, and his idea to get Huevos and Dave together was genius. Bradley is grinning from ear to ear.

"Upload it now, Mills. It's brilliant, and thank you for my credit. I don't think we'll have the same market, but—it's really kind of you."

It's not even ten in the morning, but I already feel like I've done something really quite good. I upload it and look at Bradley.

"I'd better get Dave back. Thank you so much. You're an incredible friend."

Bradley goes all businesslike and official. "That's fine. Off you go. See you soon. I'm going into the city now to film."

I've hit him with too many of the feels. I think it's time to go.

For most of the day I can't look at the vlog. The views go
up and up. By the time I check it in the afternoon, there has been, in
Lauren's terms, a meltdown. A viral sensation.

Lydia Portancia has already e-mailed.

> Millie!
>
> Obviously, the natural look is something you have opted for,
> and we will have to work with that. That's your choice. I can
> only offer advice.
>
> Great vlog. Huevos is a natural. Is anyone representing
> Huevos? I think that's a dog we could really work with
> there! Can you give me some contact deets? BTW I'm
> sending something Dave's way. A pet food company
> ADORES her.
>
> Lydia x

I've noticed that Lydia always adds kisses when she wants something.
There are loads of comments, too.

Huevos is everything

(I hope Bradley reads all these.)

More Huevos and Dave

(I think this is a really good idea.)

Huevos and Dave is my new band name

(Please become a famous musician. That would be incredible.)

My followers have gone through the roof. I feel better than I have in weeks, but a bit shallow, too. Is this all it takes for me to be happy? I can hear Mum downstairs singing "Strawberry Fields Forever" while she fixes her afternoon muesli (don't ask). I go downstairs to talk to her.

"And what are you up to today, Miss Boleyn?"

Mum calls me "Miss Boleyn" when she's in a great mood. She's got a thing about the Tudors. This is a bit random and a bit tragic, as the real Miss Boleyn was actually beheaded for being too smart for her own good. King Henry's cat also had its own suit of armor. I dare not show Dave. She might get ideas.

"I want to see Bradley, and then I think I'm going to chat with Danny for a few hours," I tell her.

Mum looks at me disappointedly. "So, to confirm, your entire day revolves around boys."

I hadn't thought about it like that, but now that Mum mentions it, it's not very feminist vlogging powerhouse, is it? If I'm being honest, it makes me worried that I might be turning into a sap. Mum goes on. "These are your holidays. Don't waste them by sitting around. Get vlogging!"

This is the first time my mum has been super-enthusiastic about the whole vlogging thing—but now she sounds like my manager. #Boss.

I think I preferred her when she thought I shouldn't be doing it.

"Think of all the vlogs you could do! You could do one every day! Go to different places! With Huevos! And Dave!"

Dave, at the sound of her name, leaps over Mum's legs and disappears back upstairs. I realize that Mum has obviously watched the new vlog, too, and is impressed.

"Okay, perhaps not Dave." Mum reassesses the situation. "But Huevos and Bradley."

The real elephant in the room is that Mum likes Bradley. He's academic, he's going to try to get to Cambridge University for science, and then he's considering a degree in disaster management. Actual disasters with hurricanes and things—not the ones you might have online.

"It's *my* vlog, Mum. All me."

"Selfridges sells Chanel, Millie. Big brands like other big brands."

Mum has an answer for everything. She's right, though. I need to visit Bradley for the second time in one day with the agent news. I think he'll lose his mind! Huevos is going to be a star!

#Surprise

On the way to Bradley's house, I think about what Mum said. Bradley lives his vlog. He starts monitoring traffic delays on Google from 6:00 a.m. He's the real deal, but he keeps it professional and he knows who he is and who his audience is. And so does Erin (more than 1,000 new subscribers). I'm still struggling, and the more I think about it, the more I get in a knot.

When I get to his room, Bradley is looking at the evening rush hour in different cities. He keeps one eye on me and one eye on congestion. The traffic patterns and maps give him a sort of joy. I try to get his head away from problems in Rome and Athens and on to my phenomenal news.

"I've got some incredible news for you. My agent wants to represent Huevos!"

Bradley does not pull the face that I thought he would. I wonder if he's just discovered a major jam in Paris or something.

"Oh," he replies. "I want Huevos to enjoy his life without the need for clicks. He'll join me in lift vlogging, but I don't want him to be a star. So, thanks, but no thanks!"

"He's a dog!" I yell.

"And I want him to stay that way," Bradley replies calmly. "He has feelings. Your cat has changed since she has become a superstar. I want Huevos to stay the way he is."

"Bradley!" I say. "Huevos thinks he's a cat. HE IS NOT NORMAL."

"There is no normal, Millie!" Bradley shouts quite sharply. "I am surprised at you for using such a terrible phrase."

I'm embarrassed, too.

"I'm sorry," I whisper.

The truth is, Bradley came up with a brilliant vlog, and now I've got to surpass myself yet again. It feels like I'm in a juicer. The pressure is always on. I've got to squeeze more good vlogs out and get rid of the pulp.

I look at Bradley. I can see that he's thinking of a way to try to make me feel better. He rubs his finger over his chin, and his glasses slip down his nose, and he creases his forehead. It's hard to read Bradley, but I'm getting to know his wide range of faces now.

"Traffic can teach you about life, Millie."

This is typical of Bradley. It all boils down to the things that he loves.

"Look at all these people on my iPad. They are all stuck, but there's nothing they can do about it. The smart ones just accept that and move on. The stupid ones are currently yelling at other drivers and increasing their risk of having a heart attack."

I don't really get what Bradley is getting at. Everyone around me seems to be growing immense philosophical systems to cope with life. I used to be the sensible one. Now, I feel like I'm constantly looking for a mind chauffeur to drive me around life.

"What's your point, Bradley?"

Bradley walks from one side of the room to the other. "My point is that you should just go with the flow!"

My flow very strongly says that Huevos should appear on my vlog on a regular basis. Dave and Huevos love each other. It's excellent pet socialization, it's fantastic for the vlog, I would get to see Bradley more and I'm scared of telling Lydia Portancia that Huevos is not for sale. I know, though, there's no point arguing with Bradley. Huevos's profile is remaining on a private locked setting.

I'm annoyed, but I try to hide it.

"Thanks, Bradley. Anyway. Got to go. I'm messaging Danny. We've arranged to speak the moment he lands."

Bradley looks at his watch. "Surely he's landed by now? Is he on the world's slowest plane?"

This is full-on Bradley snark.

"He'll still be trying to shift his body clock, you know. He might have fallen asleep on the airport transport bus."

"Or he may be seeing . . . other people," Bradley mumbles.

I don't like Bradley's tone. He's getting a bit full of himself. I need to tell him that Danny and me are 24-karat-gold SOLID.

"We really miss each other, you know, Bradley!"

Bradley raises his eyebrows. "Yeah, I bet Danny is dreaming of you right now."

This is a sarcastic comment too far. I'm wearing wedge Converse. I have extra height and extra power.

"Look, I don't pry into *your* private life. Danny and me are just FINE, thanks very much—"

Bradley interrupts me with some volume. "You can pry! I don't care. I don't have a girlfriend at the moment. This will shock you, Millie, but it's possible for a boy to be friends with a girl!"

"I know that!" I shout. "We manage it, don't we?"

Bradley pauses. "Okay, calm down, Millie."

There's "calm down" again. I am perfectly calm, thank you. I just have a magnificent handle on my own justified rage. I can see, though, that he looks a bit crestfallen after my comment. I'm not sorry to have put him in his place. If Bradley gives it, I am going to give it back.

I think Bradley knows he's gone too far. He looks at me and smiles.

"Perhaps Huevos can be a guest star sometimes."

This is a Bradley peace offering and I accept it. I give him a hug, put Dave in her carrier, and head home. Danny is due to land at 7:00 p.m. our time. I think. To be honest, I've put Toronto in the world clock section of my phone. International time zones are very confusing when you do the math in your head.

#DannyChat

When I get home, I go straight upstairs. I wait and then I wait some more. I tidy my desk multiple times and check my phone every other second. I don't even know what I'm looking at half the time. I scroll through an Instagram account about succulent plants. I have no idea why. I just like a good cactus and it's something to do.

Finally, at stupid o'clock, Danny appears on Messenger and calls me. Seeing his face is just THE BEST. It's been a very long day.

Danny grins from ear to ear and screams, "Hey, girl! I saw the vlog— it's good to see you just getting on with things! I like that!"

What does this mean? Of course, I am just getting on with things. Did he think I would vaporize without him?! I can completely cope with this situation and I don't like anyone suggesting that I can't.

Obviously, I don't say this. I'm not having our first conversation become our first transatlantic argument, so I just say, "Yeah! Bradley came up with the idea. Isn't Huevos gorgeous?"

Danny nods. "He's AMAZING. It was so good to see. I couldn't stand the thought of you just being an overemotional wreck. I don't want that guilt, really."

Overemotional wreck?! WHAT THE HELL DOES THAT MEAN? How has our first chat turned into this? Is this how Danny sees me?

"No! I'm having a good time! If anything, I toned down my natural upness a bit, as I thought you might be a bit jealous."

Danny dismisses this immediately.

"God, NO! I'm not jealous at all. No, I meant it. You've got to keep on it. You're incredible at what you do!"

On the flight home Danny seems to have devised the perfect girlfriend-annoying formula of "quite patronizing" and "not jealous at all." Don't get me wrong, I don't want an envy maniac—but I'd like him to be a little bit annoyed that I've done a joint vlog with Bradley.

After this, Danny talks. And talks. I peer down my phone as he tells me about flight attendants and vegan meals and seeing his grandma at the airport (she probably got there by rocket pack or something equally as dangerous), his house is huge, it's good to be back, and then, "anyway," he "has to go" because "there's stuff to do and friends to see and . . ."

Just as I'm about to tell him MY news, Lauren calls me and this cuts Danny off. I go to reject the call, but press ACCEPT instead. I am very annoyed at Lauren, at life, at my ludicrous fingers, and a bit at Danny, too—though I'm not quite sure why.

Lauren whispers. It's impossible to hear what she is saying. I lose my temper quite fast.

"Lauren! This better be good," I say irritably. "I was just talking to Danny for the first time. I'm going to have to put time into this, you know, to make it work!"

Lauren then does the thing that she always does when she's trying to be quiet—she shouts.

"Millie. FORGET DANNY. WE NEED TO TALK NOW."

This better be good, I think to myself. This better involve a major life crisis—illness, death, or worse.

#HotMess

"Are you sitting down?" Lauren is managing to whisper again.

"Yes," I reply. She is officially scaring the bejeezus out of me now.

Lauren takes a huge gulp.

"This morning I went to your house with my dad. You'd already gone to Bradley's place. My dad went in first and I got his toolbox from the car. When I went in your front door, I saw YOUR MUM AND MY DAD TOGETHER, AND THEY WERE KISSING!"

I take a moment. I ask Lauren if she's sure they were kissing.

Lauren does a little laugh. "Unless she was flossing his teeth, they were kissing."

I still can't get my head around all of this. I wonder if Lauren has been sleeping well recently. Tiredness can make you see things that aren't there. Also, if you spend loads of time on your phone, you can end up hallucinating. That must be what happened. There is no way on earth that my mum, who is pure strength and sense on two legs with magnificent chunky thighs that could crush steel, would go out with Lauren's dad. No offense to him, but he's like a fog. Though opposites do sometimes attract. There's a man down the street who has mismatched dogs—a Rottweiler and a Pomeranian. It does happen, but Rod and Mum would be far more bizarre than THAT.

Lauren whispers loudly, "I think my dad is listening. I've got to go. Let's speak tomorrow."

Lauren hangs up. Danny is also not there, but he's sent me a message.

> Did someone else call? Had to go anyway. Good to catch
> up. Speak SOON. D x

And then there's four hearts.

No mention of love. Just emojis.

I curl up in my bed. I'm too tired to think of anything right now. I decide not to think about Danny and not to talk to Mum. It's far too late. I'll opt for ambushing her in the morning. I know before she's had coffee she'll admit to anything.

#noway

When I wake up, there's no more messages from Danny, but Lauren has texted me.

> Millie. We are coming to your house this morning early. You watch them. THEY ARE IN PROPER LOVE.

I am not waiting to see this nonsense. I decide to tackle Mum now. I march downstairs with a bit of a face on. It's a mixture of Mum when she's in full business mode and Dave when she hasn't been fed.

Mum is making her breakfast. The kettle has boiled, but her coffee granules are dry. This is the optimum time to have a talk to her. She will be at her weakest.

"Mum," I say very calmly. "Can we have a chat?"

Mum taps her hand on the countertop. "Of course we can, darling!"

Suddenly my brain can't find the right words, so my mouth just comes out with something.

"Are you and Rod kissing?"

Mum stops tapping her hand and slowly turns around to look at me.

"Do you mean are Rod and I in a relationship? The answer is yes.

I think we are. I just want a bit of fun, Millie. It's nothing too serious. Rod is funny and spontaneous and I'm getting to live a bit. He's going to take me to a Fleetwood Mac concert. Do you know, I think I've been a bit restricted when it comes to music. Some of the stuff from pre-1991 is excellent. I don't see what the issue is. You get to hang with Lauren and I get to hang with Roddy."

Roddy?!

In this moment, I have trouble formulating a sentence. I wonder who the hell this woman is! This is not my mum. This USED to be my mum. That's why she ended up with my dad. When she was young she was a raver. Dance parties till dawn! Trance dance tunes! This WAS her. It's not her now. My mum is sensible. She has relationships with people like Gary—men who are clean and make fish pie from scratch. Not men like Rod. He vapes with a raspberry flavor! He also needs to shower (NOT my words. The words of my mum before she started kissing him), AND he is my BEST FRIEND'S DAD! There's a complete lack of imagination here.

More to the point, I'm going through one of the most stressful periods of my life and she drops this bombshell. I have grave concerns about this relationship. This may be my very sensible side reaching in to take control, but I think my sensible side is right.

Rod is a walking explosion of mess. Mum has only just finished a relationship with the world's cleanest man! How can she go so fast from the—

Before I have more time to think, Rod comes into the kitchen and says, "Hello, Millie!"

I'm not proud to tell you that I pull my exceptionally suspicious face. My eyes slide down to meet my cheeks.

Rod doesn't notice and Dave rushes into his arms. He sings a song to her. "You're a really cool cat/Feline—you're fat/Sit on the mat/Would you like a tuna-filled crepe?/Or a smoky chicken vape?"

"Millie," Mum exclaims excitedly. "You could get Rod on the vlog!"

I could not. "Hashtag Help! My Mum's Boyfriend Thinks He's John Lennon" would not be a popular upload.

No. I am not doing that. But I can think of something I *can* do.

#GourmetSnack

Lauren breezes in like nothing is happening. She is carry-ing a parcel. "Morning!" she shouts. "This was on your doorstep, Mills."

I open the parcel and realize it's the gourmet snacks Lydia Portancia promised for Dave.

I look at Lauren. She seems to be completely unfazed by everything that is going on. I, meanwhile, am standing here holding Trout Infused Gourmet Treats with a Hint of Sea Bream Broth and feeling completely bewildered.

While Rod and Mum are talking about their favorite type of peanut butter (my mum is claiming she's crunchy!) I sidle up to Lauren and sort of snarly whisper, "How do you feel about this? Aren't you completely weirded out by it?"

Lauren looks serious. She explains that she absolutely was freaked out when she saw them kissing. In fact, that's why she didn't tell me for HOURS, BUT when she sat back and thought about it, she realized it was actually a bit lovely. She looks at me very sweetly, puts her arm around me, and says, "I think you just need a bit of time. I love your mum. She loves my dad. We are sort of sisters, anyway. This is good news, isn't it?"

I scrunch up my face. Sensible Millie says, *Get over it. Don't worry about it. Mum always comes out on top.* and *Lauren is right.* Toddler Millie, who lives deep inside of me, does not agree. Toddler Millie is currently having a huge tantrum and throwing her Dancing Elmo at Rod.

At times like this, it's good to get away from the scene of conflict.

I give Lauren an arm squeeze and pry Dave from Rod's arms. I tell him I will bring her back in a minute. I take Dave and the gourmet treats to my bedroom. I do need to vlog more. Mum is right about that, even though her taste in men, and therefore all her opinions about everything, are currently under question.

#Biscuits

Dave death-stares me all the way up the stairs. She is very unhappy that I have taken her from Rod.

I sit down in my vlogging space and I check that the biscuits look really obvious on-screen. I've seen basic marketing stuff—you have to make sure that the product is king. I hold on to Dave gently but firmly and begin recording.

> Hi! Millie here! Hashtag Help my cat is a flirt and she prefers my mum's new boyfriend over me.

> I have no idea if Rod and Mum are public knowledge yet, but they're so loved up—I'm sure they won't mind.

> Yeah, so my mum has a new boyfriend. Who just happens to be the dad of my best friend. I'm not going to lie—it is odd. I only found out yesterday. They're nice people, but it's an "opposites attract" thing. That's not the problem, though. The problem is Dave.

My cat is in love with my mum's new boyfriend.

She does tricks for him that she would never do for me. She follows him around the house. She sleeps in the bathtub looking sad when he's not around. The message I am getting is—"Millie, you're not number one in my life anymore."

However, today, thanks to Feline Friends snacks I have, as you can see, Trout Infused Gourmet Treats with a Hint of Sea Bream Broth. And there's nothing my cat likes more than a cheeky luxury chow-down.

(I get some of the biscuits out and hold them in my hand. In terms of fish smell intensity, it's like holding the entire Pacific Ocean. Dave shows no interest at all. In fact, she jumps down and heads toward the door.)

That's actually quite reassuring in a way. It proves you can't totally buy the affection of things. Sometimes love is the thing that conquers.

Dave suddenly decides she IS interested, leaps onto me, buries her head into the packet and tries to claw me when I try to take the treats off her. Dave looks like she's been hypnotized.

Oh, you can buy the love of things. I think Dave might miss my boyfriend, Danny, too. We're both doing some comfort

eating! Brilliant news! Anyway, if your cat is a diva like mine, get her or him some of these!

(I rattle the treats.)

Leave your comments, and I'll see you soon.

I turn RECORD off and watch my vlog back. It feels a bit wrong—like I'm on a TV shopping channel. I can't think of a better way to do it, though, so I upload and put my phone in the front pocket of my bag. I don't want to keep refreshing for feedback about cat biscuits and it's still too early for Danny to call. I decide that I am not going to look at my phone for a bit. I am consciously uncoupling from the world for a few hours.

Dave paws me for more biscuits. I give her some. We don't do diets in this house.

#TruthAndLies

For the rest of the day, I want to tell you that I do amaz-ing productive things. I do not. I wait for Danny to call. If I even remotely hear something that sounds like a phone alert, I check mine. Mum has given Rod a whole heap of new jobs to do. Lauren and Mum think he's hilarious and, yes, at times, he is. When he develops *Dave: The Musical* with big numbers including "I'm the Star (Not Millie)" and the haunting ballad "I've Got Fleas," he is really funny. However, when you are trying to speak to your boyfriend in a completely separate time zone, things are not as fun.

Danny finally calls at about 2:00 p.m. our time. We have a good chat . . . and then he casually drops into the conversation that he is going to stay with his uncle and that his uncle is a survivalist. He then explains that his uncle lives in the middle of nowhere in a log cabin that he built with no running water.

Even the thought of it gives me a tight chest.

Danny, though, "really can't wait to go" to "catch fish and watch the raccoons."

His grandma is going, too, as she likes to hunt.

And he will have no phone connection. For a few days.

"So, what shall we do?" I ask.

Danny looks at me with a very confused face. "We just won't talk for a few days. We often were like that when I lived near you! It's no different!"

I nod, but inside I am thinking very differently. Danny just seems to be picking up his Canadian life where he left off. I know I should be fine with that, but where do I fit into it all? I don't think I can go to stay in a house in the middle of a forest, unless I can take my Zen Loo with me.

A horrible thought creeps into my head. *Is this REALLY going to work?* Do I want it to? I'm not really a hanging-around type of girl.

Put the thought away, Millie. Positive thinking. Yes. I can make our relationship work. If Rod and Mum can, anyone can!

#Honesty

Later, to cheer myself up a bit, I look at the comments on my latest vlog. There are loads of them and thousands of views.

#DAVE. Just make it Dave #DaveFan

(She is actually physically incapable of doing vlogs on her own.)

This is amazing. You have yourself one special cat there.

(I know. I hope no one tries to kidnap her.)

CAAATTTTTTTTTTTTTTT!!!!!!

(Yes, Dave is a cat.)

Is the cat for real? Or a puppet

(I can't be bothered with these ones.)

Kummerspeck!

(I look this up. It is German for "grief bacon." It's their word for excess weight caused by emotional eating. Don't try to body-shame my cat! If she wants to have a few extra treats because she might miss Danny, she can.)

There's also an e-mail from Lydia Portancia.

MILLIE!

The company LOVES the vlog and they ADORE Dave. Pets are often resistant to anything new. Dave has spoken to a lot of other cat people who will get that. I think this is the start of something BIG for her. Perhaps a corporate sponsorship!

Reading everything back, it's a lot of Dave is doing really good and not a lot of me is doing really good.

I can't be jealous of my cat's career. That is too tragic.

My phone vibrates and I see it's Aunty Teresa.

Millie! Are you busy? Come over! I have a great idea!

Right now, with Lauren and Rod devising *Dave: The Musical* in the bathroom, and Danny planning to live amongst the mooses, this seems like a good escape.

(I have no idea what the real plural of moose is and I can't take another thing onboard my head today. I can only buffer information from now on.)

#TeresaNO

When I get to Granddad's house, Teresa is waiting by the front door and waving excitedly. It's good to get silly Teresa back. Since she's been into medicine, she's been all about hemorrhagic fevers and mosquitoes. She beckons me into the front room. She looks at me nervously. I can see she is dying to tell me something.

"You know we were talking about your vlog being a bit too serious? I thought about that. I have found a way to totally open up a side of yourself that other people haven't seen. It introduces vulnerability, yet your strength and your humor, too."

I stare at her suspiciously. "Have you seen my vlog recently? I'm doing loads of funny stuff. I've decided funny is me—a bit."

Teresa starts to look sheepish. "No, I haven't seen it. I've been too busy working out a strategy for you. I was thinking of something extra-fun for your fans."

"They're not fans. They are subscribers," I say firmly. I can't deal with having "fans." Too heavy on my head.

"Anyway," Teresa continues, "I hope I've done the right thing. I was going through a really old phone and I spotted a video I made from about eight years ago. When you were little."

My stomach goes full washing-machine.

"It was so cute, I just uploaded it onto your vlog! You were still logged in to my laptop. I've done the right hashtags and everything!"

Breathe, Millie. That's what my brain says. Finally, my mouth works.

"You've put it on my vlog page?"

Teresa looks down and shifts from side to side. "Yeah, it's that time at Christmas."

My eyes go wide. Please no. *Please NO!*

How can one woman cause so much damage in forty minutes?! Teresa can read my reaction. She grabs hold of my arms and pleads, "I was just thinking of you, Millie! I thought people would see you in a whole new way!"

I open up my phone, and there it is. Teresa has even labeled it to fit in with what I do.

#Help me, I've dropped the baby Jesus and Mary is understandably furious at me.

Teresa starts to do that thing when you know someone is going to be furious at you. She starts blurting out a really poor defense of her actions with a fake smile.

"You had one job in the nativity play! Just to pass the baby Jesus to Mary. And you dropped it! Incredible scenes, Millie. I still think about it! You've already got lots of views!"

I surprise myself. I can't get cross. I know Teresa hasn't got a malicious bone in her entire skeleton. It is very embarrassing, but it's a bit funny, too. Also, it's Sarah Browning as the Angel Gabriel telling me off for dropping the doll. She was horrible to everyone when she was six. I don't suppose it matters if the world knows me as the cat girl who drops babies.

"You're not angry, are you, Millie?"

Teresa breaks my train of thought. I tell her I'm not, give her a hug, and log myself out of her laptop. I also realize I need to change all my passwords to things that she could never, ever guess. Davel was a bit weak. I promise Teresa that I'll come and see her and Granddad tomorrow. I've got nothing else to do. My boyfriend is up a tree, my mum is in love, and my best friend is trying to get on Broadway with a musical based on my cat.

Everything is completely normal.

The last few months have been crazy. I don't think I can handle another big emotional thing. I need the opposite. Someone factual and down to earth.

I text Bradley.

Coffee?

Bradley gets back to me straightaway.

Yes! Come to mine.

#Oasis

Bradley's house is always an oasis of calm in a world gone
wild. He manages to keep on top of everything I'm doing, too. When I
get to his room, he's already seen Teresa's handiwork.

He grins at me. He has a buck-teeth thing going on, but it works.

"That was brave, Millie," he says very factually.

I explain that it wasn't me who uploaded it. This makes him laugh
a lot. I notice that his voice is getting deeper. Men really do get the best
deal when it comes to hormones. I should vlog about it, and get it sponsored by a hot water bottle manufacturer.

"You know what, Bradley?" I confess. "It's good to have something
that's just about me. It's mainly been about Dave. I feel like Dave's
spare part sometimes. I know it's pathetic being jealous of my own cat,
but . . ."

I notice Bradley is shaking with laughter and I realize how ridiculous
I sound.

"Bradley! Take this a bit seriously!" I say. "I just want to be as legendary as my pet!"

I can hear that I have gone full spoon. I decide to shut up and get
Bradley on his favorite subject.

"How's the lifts, anyway?"

"Oh, you know, up and down." And then he winks.

This is a good bad joke. Bradley is dry like the desert. It is, in my opinion, the greatest of all the humors. Most boys of his age are still laughing at their own body gas. Bradley has gone up many levels. We spend the rest of the afternoon talking about technology, comparing vlogs, and giggling at Huevos.

But NO. He's JUST a friend. There will be no plot twist. But, when I'm with him, I do tend to laugh a lot more and eat a lot more, which I think is always a great sign of being with another human (or cat).

#Vlog

When I get home, I have gone viral again. Not exactly me,
but little me. Other people are now sharing their embarrassing school
play stuff too—#nativityfails is trending. Teresa is actually a genius,
and I text her to tell her. I'm very lucky to have the family that I have.
Perhaps I don't tell them as much as I should.

I feel this way, all warm and fuzzy, until I find Mum in my room
inflating the airbed.

"Millie!" she says excitedly. "Rod and Lauren are having their
house done up by specialists. They've found asbestos in the walls!
The thing is, it's really a big job, so I've asked if he wants to stay here!
And Lauren can stay with you! It'll be FUN! It's only for a day or
two!"

It's that "fun" word again.

I realize I'm being a grump. I love Lauren and I need to be more
patient. Plus, selfishly, I know having her around will take my mind off
Danny not being around.

Lauren crashes into the bedroom and starts shouting, "Isn't this the
best holiday EVER?!"

I nod and give her a hug. She puts her bag onto my bed. "Do you mind if I sleep here, Millie? I don't really sleep well on air!"

I nod. To be honest, I feel so tired that I could sleep in a hedge.

#Discoveries

The next morning, I have discovered the following things about my best friend:

- Lauren doesn't sleep well on normal beds, either.
- Lauren likes late-night talking. She asked me about the Big Bang Theory. I said I didn't know, as I couldn't believe there was just this huge explosion and everything happened. There must be a God. Or something. Or someone. Lauren didn't mean the theory. She meant the show (I've been spending too much time with Bradley). She then told me all the jokes from all the seasons of the show ever.
- She fell asleep telling me a joke, then woke herself up again laughing.
- Lauren sings in her sleep and buzzes like a bee. It's a bit freaky.
- When Lauren wakes up in the morning, she does an over-dramatic yawn that sounds like an earthquake.
- I am officially VERY tired. Lauren dashes downstairs for breakfast very early.

I check my phone. Lydia Portancia has TEXTED me.

> Millie. WONDERFUL VIRAL WORK! Please make sure that
> you have a valid passport. If you don't, please get one. Ask
> your mum if she has one, too. Will have news soon!

I know I have one. I shout down to Mum and ask her if she has one, too. Mum responds with "Yes! Why?"

When I shout back, "I don't know!" Mum just laughs. Rod giggles, too. This house has become very silly very fast. Going to Granddad's house is going to be a sensible relief.

I can't believe I'm even saying that when Aunty Teresa lives there.

#FirstAid

When Granddad answers his front door, he is bleeding heavily from his head. Only he's not. It's ketchup.

Granddad groans, "Don't ask! Your aunty is practicing bandages. The sauce is there for authenticity, apparently."

Teresa jumps up and down when she sees me. "Millie! How fantastic are me and you as a TEAM! We are VIRAL! I was so pleased to see it go big. Can I bandage you, by the way?"

Everyone is very excited about me going viral, but now it just seems like something I have to do. It doesn't feel like something to celebrate—just my job. I think I have lost the "fun" of it. The real fun. Not the fun that people force on you.

I sit on the couch and let Teresa practice putting my arm in a sling. She's not very good at it. She nearly dislocates my shoulder. It's at this point that my phone decides to ring. I can see it's Lydia Portancia, but I can only use my left arm to pick up my phone. I drop it at first and Teresa has to hold it up to my ear. This sight makes Granddad cry with laughter.

"Millie!" Lydia yells. "I have some incredible news! Tourism Toronto is very interested in giving you and your mum a trip to Canada to see

Danny! It'll be a weekend package. In a few weeks. You go there, you see Danny, you see some sights. Young love! Fantastic places! You take some footage. Send it back. We will edit it and put it together for you for vlog! How does that sound?!"

It sounds so incredible I can't believe it's my life. I am being flown to see my boyfriend in a foreign city!

"Are you there?!" Lydia shouts.

"Sorry!" I reply. "Yes! I'll obviously have to ask my mum, but I think it will be a yes. YES!"

Lydia whoops with excitement. "Also, we're going to start putting ads in your vlogs. That means money. Things have gotten BIG, Millie, and it's down to you. You have made this happen. Well, you and Dave! I'll give your mum a call just to check everything is okay with her!"

When I hang up from Lydia, Teresa starts jumping up and down and hollering. Granddad hugs me and tells me how proud he is of me. "You'll be wanting to get home, Millie, to tell your mum. She'll be thrilled! You know, when you started all this nonsense, I thought, 'that'll go nowhere,' but you've proved me wrong!"

Teresa suddenly pulls a face of horror.

"Who will look after Dave? I volunteer! I can practice some basic tourniquets on her!"

"She's a cat, Teresa!" Granddad yells.

"There are many similarities between us and felines, Dad!" Teresa says with a sniff.

"Like what?" I giggle.

Teresa thinks for a time.

"Legs!"

The evil part of my brain says if I leave Dave with Rod, she'll forget me by the time I get back and may not ever love me again. I tell Teresa she can look after her, and I fully express this insecurity by eating a very large sandwich that Granddad made me.

Just as I'm about to polish it off, Mum calls me.

"Millllliiiiiieee!!" she screams. "We are going to Canada! You clever, clever girl! I am SO proud of you, we are going to have such a good time! I can't wait! I bet you can't, either!"

"No, I can't," I tell her.

Everyone is so excited. *Why do I feel so sick?*

And how can I tell Danny that we are coming to visit him when he's living in a tree?

#Lumberjack

When I get home, Mum is singing Celine Dion songs with Rod. They don't notice me at first because they are too busy belting out the theme from *Titanic*. I walk into the lounge just as they are wailing that their hearts will go on. When Mum sees me, she tries to pick me up and spin me around. Lauren runs in and there's a semi–group hug thing going on within seconds.

It's great, but inside of me I am feeling very quivery. I ask to talk to Mum on my own.

"Mum." I sigh. "I'm just going to say this. Part of me doesn't want to go. Every time I think about flying, vlogging abroad, and even seeing Danny, I feel like I'm going to puke. My head goes dizzy. I feel like I can't breathe. I feel . . ."

"You're having a little panic attack," Mum says very matter-of-factly, "and that's completely normal. This is a huge thing for someone with a brain like yours. And like mine. I'm nervous, too. But I know if we don't go, we'll regret it forever! It's a free weekend trip abroad. You'll be with me! And Danny!"

"I can't even tell him," I say. "He's with some uncle who is off the grid. Do I vlog it now, or wait, or—"

"Take a deep breath, close your eyes for five seconds, and vlog it now!" Mum yells. "It's YOUR trip. YOU have earned it. Let's enjoy it. Commit to it now! Do it, Mills! Danny will be thrilled when he finds out!"

Mum always makes me feel better. She drives me mad but, essentially, she is magnificent. I punch the air and run upstairs. I can do this. I can TOTALLY do this. I think.

I collect Dave from underneath the radiator and go to my desk.

#Trip

I am nervous about doing this vlog. It is HUGE news. Before
I press RECORD, I take Mum's advice and take a deep breath in and out.
While I'm doing this, Dave tries to put her paw over my nostril. Perhaps
she *is* training to be a killer cat. Finally, once I've got her paw off my
face, I'm ready to start.

> Hi! Millie here! A quick one, but an amazing one! Tourism
> Toronto has seen me moaning about missing my boyfriend
> and they've seen Dave pretend to be a beaver AND . . .
> Hashtag Help! They have invited us to CANADA!!
>
> When I say "us," I mean me and my mum. Sadly, Dave can't
> come because if we take her there we can't take her back
> for months. She'd have to go into quarantine, which is this
> place where they check animals don't have something
> horrid called rabies. Don't google it. It's awful.

Dave absolutely seems to understand this. She buries her head into
my chest. This makes me feel completely emotional, but I carry on.

225

ANYWAY, we're only going for a few days. We'll be seeing . . .

And I realize I don't know exactly what we will be seeing.

. . . all Toronto stuff like the big waterfall, AND I will get to
see Danny. Here's the weird thing: You'll be finding out I'm
going before he does because he's currently with his uncle
who thinks humanity is doomed. To cut a long story short,
he doesn't have a phone on him and this will be a TOTAL
surprise. Anyway, if you've got any thoughts on what I
should see or shouldn't see, leave it in the comments. And
I'll see you from Canada soon!

As I press STOP, I realize that Mum has been listening at the door.
She rushes in and says, "Millie. We need to talk."

"Okay," I say. This is a bit of a mood change.

"I don't mind you mentioning me and Rod. I don't mind you saying I used to have anxiety, and that I still have to manage it—I'm not
ashamed of that—but under no circumstances may you EVER show
anyone my passport photo."

Though this makes me laugh, I can see Mum is deadly serious, so
I promise her that I won't—though, obviously, I really want to see it.
Perhaps she had really bad hair.

When Mum leaves, I upload the video. It's official: We are going to
Canada. I hope Danny is out of the forest by the time we go. I'm not really
a camping kind of person. I get scared when I can't use a hair dryer.

#NoDave?

The next morning, I wake up and look at my phone. I have seventeen missed calls and it's only 6:23 a.m.

Lauren is very grumpy. "Your phone keeps giving out bad blue light. It's kept me awake."

"I'm sorry, Loz," I reply. "It was on silent. It just wasn't on dark. Danny has tried to call me loads of times. He told me he was in the middle of nowhere without reception!"

Lauren is still half awake. "Try calling him back when it's morning!"

I don't even try to explain to her that it IS morning. I go to the bathroom and I try to call Danny back, but there's no reply. I try again just for luck, and he answers.

He seems a bit stressed.

"Hello, Millie! Hang on . . . Hang on. Just let me go to this washing line. Hang on. It's night here. Hang on. There's no point in doing video. It won't work. Is it true you're coming here? Mum rang the store in the next village to us!"

"Yes!" I yelp. "In a couple of weeks! Tourism Toronto is paying for it. We can see each other! You will be back in Toronto, won't you?"

Danny goes quiet and then replies, "Yeah! I should be. That's great!

227

Anyway, I've got to go. It's not really safe out here. Bears! I'll send you my home address, though, when I'm back in civilization. Bye, Mills."

And he hangs up.

I stand by the sink for a few minutes and think about what just happened.

Why did he tell me he wouldn't have phone reception when he does? Why wasn't he as excited as everyone else when I told him we were going to Canada? Why have I got this terrible feeling in my stomach that things are not quite right?

Mum knocks on the door. "Hurry up, will you, Millie?!"

I unlock it and step outside. Mum can see I'm wearing a frowny face and asks me if I'm okay. I tell her I'm just tired. That's partly true, but I'm mainly wondering if my boyfriend is already seeing someone else and if she also lives in the Canadian wilderness. Perhaps she's been there all this time—waiting for him and carving animals from wood. Or something.

When I go back in the bedroom, Lauren murmurs, "Did you speak to Bradley? Sorry, I mean Danny. I get mixed up in the morning."

"Yeah," I reply. "He could speak to me. I don't think he was that excited, though."

Lauren wakes up incredibly quickly. "Why?" she yells.

"Just a feeling I get. I think there might be someone else, Loz!"

"No, Mills!" Lauren shouts. "He loves you. You can tell. I think he was just distracted by the—"

"Bears." I finish her sentence.

Lauren brightens up. "Exactly! Bears! And they are scary. That's why the Polish army had one in World War Two!"

As Lauren is back on her favorite bit of trivia ever, I check the reaction to the Canada vlog. Some of it is annoying.

I only watch this for Dave! I don't think I'll watch Canada if she's not there.

(I can't smuggle her in my hand luggage!)

That's a long way to go for such a short time.

(As Mum says, we don't turn down a free holiday! We will deal with the jet lag.)

Toronto has the world's longest road. Can you check it out for me, please, and get some footage?

(This is from Bradley. Yes, of course I will.)

Whatever anyone says, Canada is happening. I'm just worried that Danny and I might not be.

#PlaneAnxiety

For the next few weeks, Mum and I prepare for our trip. I don't have much time to worry about anything, as it's all visas, phone calls, itineraries, Lydia Portancia panicking, and Mum packing and repacking about fifty times. Danny sends me lots of messages, and we speak a few times. He acts fine. Mum thinks I was expecting a bit too much. She says when I see him, we will just jigsaw together and it will all fit. I think she's wrong. I think there's something just not right. I think Zan might not be . . .

I don't know. Yin and Yang. Zan and . . . Millie. It's just not the same.

I get myself so wound up about this that I don't vlog, and I barely sleep. It's tragic. I also decide that seeing Bradley is a bad idea because I worry it might confuse me before I go.

Lydia Portancia tries to be understanding by suggesting I save all my energy for Canada. Besides, she's "very busy with her other clients" like Erin. Who is now the spokeswoman for a spray-on hair dye. Lydia uses "I'm busy with other clients" like a punishment, but I can't quite explain why.

Eventually, it's time for me and Mum to leave for the airport. Rod and Mum kiss in the street, Loz makes a sick noise, Granddad sends me a kiss by text, Aunty Teresa reminds me to stay away from stagnant water, and Bradley sends me a message.

Don't forget my road

With a heart.

I was right not to date him. He is confusing.

When we get to the airport, I remember that they are the worst places on EARTH for anyone with anxiety. There are the endless questions: *Am I carrying anything suspicious? Did I pack my bags myself?* (No, my mum did. Fifty times.) There's beeps, random swabs, and X-rays. Mum can see that I'm nervous. She leans over and whispers, "Remember, we all have fear. It's the management of that fear that counts!" She then organizes the check-in line and lets a woman with small children go in front of us. Everyone else tuts, but Mum doesn't care. She winks at me and says quietly, "If I keep busy doing the right thing, I forget my worry. Top tip!"

When we finally board the plane, Mum goes a bit holiday happy. She asks for champagne before she even sits down and then, unbelievably, the flight attendant brings one to her! Once we've taken off, I settle down and try to sleep. I can't quite believe I am 36,000 feet in the air. In fact, I try not to think I'm in the air at all. I focus on landing. And my hotel bed. In Canada.

#OhCanada

The next day I wonder, *Is this the next day?* **and** *Is* **this** *Canada?* There's a great word for this feeling—"discombobulated."

I wake up at 3:00 a.m. The hotel air conditioning is whirring and Mum is doing her semi-snore. Jet lag is real and I can't sleep. The hotel wireless is rubbish and Mum refused to make my phone international-roaming friendly. Therefore, I start to overthink everything. Like air conditioning. Teresa told me about something called Legionnaires' disease. It lives in air conditioning. It gives you pneumonia, but you just think you've got a bad cold until it's too late.

I fall asleep with this thought till I wake up again two hours later. I feel like a zombie and I may have a deadly illness that will kill me with a hacking cough but IT IS GENUINELY GREAT TO BE HERE!

Mum springs out of bed. She travels for work and seems to have complete resistance to tiredness, jet lag, and probably Legionnaires' disease. "Come on, Millie!" she yells. "WE ARE IN CANADA!!"

In the hotel lobby next/this/WHATEVER morning, we meet our guide. She is a permanently happy woman called Cindy with bright red hair and a clipboard. She greets us like we've known her for years.

"Ms. Porter! Millie! Good to see you here! We've got such a packed schedule! The first day you are going to Niagara Falls and up the CN Tower! And then tomorrow, Millie, of course, there'll be time for you to see your partner!"

My partner. That sounds very old.

"Now," Cindy adds, "is there anything you want to do?"

I think of Bradley. "I'd like to see the world's longest street, please!"

Cindy looks odd for a moment. "Yeah! We can do that! Anything else?"

Mum shakes her head. "Not for me. I just can't wait to get going!"

"Okay, then," Cindy says excitedly. "Let's go to the CN Tower!"

#Tower

There's one thing everyone in the world should know about the CN Tower. It's very, very high. I know towers are normally not short, but this one is HUGE. I stand at the bottom of it and look up.

"Are we going up there?" I ask.

"Oh, you're not just going up!" Cindy shouts. "You're going to hang off the edge."

"Yeah, of course we are!" I laugh. I hope Canadians get sarcasm.

"I've read about this," Mum blurts excitedly.

I have not read about it, and I go very pale indeed.

"Mum, I can't do heights. You know I can't. Plus, I'm too young!"

"Oh no, you're not, honey," Cindy squeals excitedly. "You've just made the age limit. See how you feel when you get to the top!"

When we get to the top, I don't feel any different. We agree that Mum is going to hang off the edge, Cindy is going to film her, and I will concentrate on the words.

Hello, Millie here in Canada and Hashtag Help! We are up the CN Tower. I am going to level with you. I just can't do

234

what Mum is about to do, as my anxiety level even being up here is just stupid, BUT the view is incredible! Look!

Cindy spins the phone around. Toronto is STUNNING VON DER STUNNING!

I am now going to watch as my mum hangs off the edge of this tower. It's 553 meters up in the air. She will be attached by some ropes and other hopefully very strong stuff.

I look out and Mum hangs off the edge and waves. She's all rigged up and looks incredible. She looks into the camera and says, "I LOVE CANADA!!"

If you want to come to Canada and you want Hashtag Help to hang off an incredibly high building, you can find it here. I mean, you might die!

Mum shouts, "You won't! It's completely safe and totally exhilarating!"

You won't die! In fact, I bet if Dave fell from here, she'd still land the right way up! Don't worry, she's not here, we won't try it!

Cindy puts her thumb up. "Great! That's a wrap on the tower!"

When my mum comes back in, she gives me a huge hug. She is buzzing with excitement. "What's next?!" she yells.

Cindy's eyes go wide. "Niagara Falls!"

#Falls

When we get to Niagara Falls, I realize that not even Erin
Breeler could manage to look fashionable in a disposable clear poncho.
It is beautiful, though, even though I don't like water. We REALLY get
wet and I do an amazing vlog from behind the waterfall. Cindy says it's
fantastic and that she's going to forward all of what we've done today to
Lydia Portancia for her to edit.

There's just one final place to visit.

"Here's Yonge Street," Cindy says, clearly unimpressed. She gets the
phone out and starts filming. Mum smiles at me. She knows that this is
important to me.

> I'm doing this vlog to Hashtag Help my friend Bradley. He
> wanted me to visit Yonge Street, which, for you transport
> geeks, is the longest road in the world. Some people say
> it's just a street because a highway takes over, but anyway,
> for you, Bradley, here is an incredibly long road.
>
> With stuff.

This ends on the border with the USA, I think, but I can't
be bothered to walk that far, as tomorrow I am visiting my
boyfriend. YAY!

"And that's a wrap!" Cindy shouts. "What a great day! Well done both! Let's go back to the hotel for some eats."

#RuinMyPrawn

Back at the hotel we eat a huge plate of seafood. I'm just about to demolish a prawn when Danny messages me.

> See you tomorrow. Can't wait. You won't be vlogging, will
> you? X

Why doesn't Danny want me to vlog? I show the message to Mum. Mum raises her eyebrows. "He does realize how we got here? I mean, you'll have to do something! Tourism Toronto paid for everything and Cindy is a single mother!"

Cindy nods. "I can do pieces with your mum from the spots that we visit and you can just do a little vlog at the end about what a beautiful day you've had with your boyfriend and how much you love Toronto. And if you can slip in that Maple Airlines brings people together, that would be good!"

I think I can do all that. I can't wait to see Danny, but I still have my doom stomach. What if we see each other and realize we were a huge mistake?

I eat another squid ring. That's the sensible thing to do. Until I remember Lauren told me that cephalopods are really intelligent and can open jars with their tentacles. Even when Lauren isn't with me, her trivia is. I eat some salad instead. Lettuce deserves to die.

#CoolMum

The next morning (it is the next morning today!), I wake
up and read the comments on our first Canadian vlog.

> **Your mum is seriously cool**

(I know.)

> **#Feministwarrior**

(I know they mean Mum.)

> **#MissDave**

(So do I.)

> **I love your relationship. It's like you are mother and**
> **daughter but also friends.**

(I think we are.)

Bit ungrateful Millie! Hang off the tower! Good old Mum!

(I do regret it now. And yes, good old Mum.)

Thanks for my road x

(Bradley!)

Basically, my mum is a powerhouse, I am pathetic, and Bradley is lovely.

There. Right there. That's the feeling that makes me feel guilty, that's the feeling that makes me confused. And that's the feeling that I have when Cindy says, "It's time to go and see your boyfriend, Millie!"

It's time. I get out the present that I've brought Danny (a multipack of his favorite chips), and we get in the car.

#Danny

We drive forever. Eventually we find Danny's house. It's
HUGE, like everything else in Toronto. I never realized Danny's family
was this rich. Not that it makes a difference to me, but he must have
thought we lived in a shed compared to him.

I see Danny in what I think is his bedroom window. He smiles from
ear to ear and races down to greet me. His mum opens the front door.
"Millie!" she shouts. "Welcome to Canada!" Mrs. Trudeau gives my
mum and Cindy the thumbs-up sign, they drive off, and the next thing I
know, it's just me and Danny.

He looks LUSH. He gives me a hug and it lasts forever, but it's the sort
of hug that you give to a friend. We kiss, too, but it all feels a bit wrong.

It's not Danny feeling this. It's me. I still like Danny loads, but . . .

"This is hard, isn't it?" Danny says.

I put my head down. "Yeah, but why? We were so good together, and
ever since you've been here, it's just felt like you've . . ."

"Changed?" Danny says.

"Yeah!" I reply. "But I don't think you have. I think I might have!
Which may make me horrible and selfish, but I don't think I want to go
out with someone I can only see once a year."

Danny does a half laugh.

"Millie. I have never met anyone like you, and I think you're great, but . . ."

I get it. For the first time I understand what my stomach had been trying to tell me. I think I had to be with Danny in the flesh for the right words to appear in my head.

"This can't really work, can it, Danny? You're Zan and I'm not. Plus you're Zan on another continent."

"No," Danny says sadly, "it can't."

I stand up and look out of the window.

We are both very sensible. Far too sensible.

"I wish I'd saved this conversation till later, though. Now we've got eight hours of being together and knowing that we are breaking up. Sorry!"

With that, Danny and I both start to cry. Eventually, after a huge sob on each other's shoulders, Danny says, "Look! Why don't I take you around the neighborhood? We can still have a good day! I can show you some sights. We can still be . . . friends!"

And that's what we do. Danny shows me his school, his skate park, and the ice hockey rink. We talk a bit about his uncle (scary, but would be good in a war), we talk about bears (scary, and also good in a war— LAUREN WAS RIGHT!), we laugh about lots of things, and we eat noodles.

But when my mum eventually comes to pick me up, Danny and I are still splitting up.

"Bye, Mills," he says on his porch. "Let's still talk, but, you know."

I do know.

"Danny, I have to ask. Is there anyone else?"

243

Danny looks at his feet and shuffles them a bit. "Nah. Just you. Honestly. I've been in a forest for ages. No girls there and, anyway, after this, I'm going to take my time."

I sigh. "Me, too."

Danny waves me good-bye, I get in the car, Mum says, "How was it, darling?" and I start to sob.

#Crying

It's very embarrassing, crying in front of someone you
don't really know, but Cindy is very good about it and hands me lots of
tissues.

Mum and Cindy let me cry all the way back to the hotel. When we
are finally back in our room, Mum gives me a huge hug and lets me cry
some more.

"I don't know why I'm so upset. It was a joint decision," I tell her.

Mum cuddles me even tighter. "Millie, that was SO brave of you. Forget
hanging off of a building! You had the sense to realize that something wasn't
working and YOU SAID SO. Do you know how many people go through
life not saying what they want?! They put up with things for YEARS. But
no, not you—YOU are a feminist warrior—not me!"

That may be true, but how do you do a vlog thanking the company
and building them up when you've had the worst time ever?

I ask Mum this question, and she says, "Don't worry. I went white-
water rafting today! They've got more than enough. And when we get
home and you feel better—you can do something then! Let's have a
great last day just doing what we want!"

My mum is amazing. I'm glad everyone on YouTube realizes it.

#Blur

The rest of the Canada trip goes by in a blur. We shop on the last day, we say good-bye to Cindy, and we fly home. This is a really ungrateful thing to say, but it all feels a bit flat. Lydia Portancia says that Tourism Toronto is really happy and that it's "just the beginning" for me, but on our first day back at home, there's one tiny problem. I don't feel like vlogging. Ever again.

Not even Dave leaping into my arms or Loz saying that she's missed me so much that she's had "physical leg pains" makes me feel any more like doing it. I don't feel like telling the world that Danny and I are no more—so I don't. I know I will get trolled by people telling me that I was "batting way out of my league" or that I'm a "spoiled brat." Honestly, I wish someone would just vlog it for me.

I do the sensible thing. I go to bed. My phone is downstairs, and I don't even care. It can stay there tonight. I have my cat, and that's all I need.

#HelpHijack

When I wake up the next day, I feel a bit better. It's nice to be back in my own bed, and I feel like I can cope with life a bit more. I feel like I could even vlog. I go downstairs to check my phone, but then something very strange happens.

Mum karate-chops it away from my hands.

"What are you doing?" I shout.

Mum looks down. "Millie, I had a glass of wine last night and it made me feel a bit brave. I did something. I think it was the right thing to do, but . . . have a look!"

Mum holds up my phone.

It's on my vlogging account and there's a new upload on it that I didn't do.

Mum grimaces and presses PLAY. The video starts. It's Mum sitting on the couch with Dave. She starts talking.

> Hashtag Hello! Sorry, I mean Hashtag Help! Hello, it's
> Millie's mum here. Look, Millie is a bit upset. Can I be can-
> did? She and Danny have broken up. There was no drama.

There was no infidelity. They were just two young people who live miles away from each other.

Look, I'm old-fashioned, but generally in relationships it's really good to be able to see people. To hug them. To kiss them. To talk to them. This *(she points to the phone)* world is great, but you need to catch some germs, people!!

Loads of you are going to be terrified of the real world. I was hospitalized with anxiety when I was young. It's not a new thing to be scared, you know. And things don't always work out with boys. Or girls. Gay or straight, it doesn't matter. If other humans are involved, it can get messy.

Dave and I get each other, don't we, Dave?

Mum strokes Dave—and pulls a disgusted face at the amount of hair that she pulls out, but carries on.

Anyway. That's it. My daughter is lovely. Leave comments if you like, but I'm not going to read them. I've got a new boy-friend, and I go back to work in a few days.

Mum stares at me. I think she wants me to say something, but I don't know what to say. Then, all of a sudden, I go off like a volcano and my lava starts to flow.

#Fury

"What did you think you were doing, Mum? You hijacked my vlog and now everyone knows that me and Danny have split up!"

Mum knows she's stepped over the line and gets all shouty.

"BUT, it means that you don't have to announce it to everyone and— read the comments—everyone thinks you and me are amazing!"

I put my head in my hands. "It's MY vlog, Mum. You even said you weren't going to read the comments and you have. It wasn't YOUR news to announce. This vlog has been about ME being ME and Dave being Dave. That's what I've been fighting for! You were tired. You had a Chardonnay, and then you got brave, and—"

Just as I'm getting in my stride, Aunty Teresa calls.

"Ignore it," Mum yells. "This is important!"

I remember where I was. "Yeah. You basically shouldn't have done it."

Teresa calls again. We ignore it again.

"Millie, it's not all about you. I hate all this fake stuff on these places. It helps no one. In fact—"

Teresa calls again.

"Teresa, WHAT?!" Mum yells into the phone.

I hear Teresa say something quite quietly.

"What?" Mum says.

I can tell it's something serious, so I go to ask. Mum does the scary-face-flappy-arm thing that tells you to shut up.

She finally finishes the call. She goes to pick up her car keys.

"Okay, Millie, sweetheart. Teresa thinks Granddad has had a stroke."

"A stroke? Doesn't your brain bleed or something?" I ask.

"Yes. It can," Mum says very calmly. "Teresa noticed his speech was slurred and his right side was weak. She worked out that he hadn't been to anywhere tropical recently and probably didn't have an exotic disease. Teresa decided that he was probably having a stroke."

"Is he going to be okay?" I whisper.

"Honestly, I don't know. Let's go to the hospital," Mum says. She puts her arm around me and we get into the car. An argument about a vlog seems pretty stupid right now.

#ɑandƐ

On the way to the hospital, every song on the radio is annoying and Mum and I hardly say a word to each other. When we get to the emergency room, Aunty Teresa is there and she looks terrible. We both give her a huge hug and sit down in the bright-green plastic chairs. I text Dad, Loz, and Bradley. It's funny who pops into your head at times like these.

We wait for a long time—there is lots of coughing and sneezing. Teresa tries to diagnose everyone and Mum gets annoyed. "I was just trying to take my mind off everything," Teresa says sadly.

Mum holds her hand and says, "I understand. Sorry."

Eventually a doctor comes out. She is lovely. She gathers us around and says, "It does look like a minor stroke. Who was with him?"

Teresa raises her hand. "Well, it was your quick thinking that got him here so we could get him stable. Well done."

I smile at Teresa. She's genuinely a medical expert.

"It'll be a long road," the doctor explains, "but he should be okay. He'll need physiotherapy. Some tough talking. It's not going to be easy. He's already tried to discharge himself twice. Until he realized that his leg was unable to work. He also kept calling me a nurse, but I put that down to him having a minor brain injury."

I know this is not the reason, but I don't say anything as I don't want to "out" Granddad as a sexist. He is trying. He's just from a generation of men who were told that women should stay at home and believed it. Probably because it suited them.

"Don't worry," Mum says. "We'll make sure he does as he's told. Can we see him?"

The doctor thinks for a moment. "Give us about twenty minutes to get him really comfortable, then yes."

In that time, Lauren messages me with every link to every page about strokes in the history of the Internet. She also texts me about stroke rehabilitation. Apparently, it's good to keep the brain active with trivia.

I think I'll be seeing even more of Lauren than normal. And that's a great thing.

#FINE

Twenty minutes later, Granddad is telling us he is fine even though we have to scratch his nose for him because his arm isn't working properly. Dad has called about sixteen times and Aunty Teresa keeps telling him that he doesn't need to come back from Ibiza. Granddad is going to be fine, Teresa says, because she has it "completely taken care of." She tells us that she is going to use "conventional therapy and some herbal remedies."

Even through a brain injury, Granddad manages to pull the face of "not on your life, Teresa."

Granddad looks at me. His voice is slurred, but you can still understand him. "Come here, Mills. I can see that you're worried . . . don't be. I can't promise you that I'll be around forever but I don't think I'm going tonight. And don't worry, I won't let Teresa finish me off, either!"

This makes me laugh. It seems wrong to be happy at a time like this, but my giggle makes Granddad smile.

"Millie," he whispers, "can you bring me my book of flags, please? I'd like to make sure I can still beat you while I'm stuck in here."

I nod.

"We'll go now," Mum says. "You need to rest, Granddad, and Teresa is a great nurse."

Teresa beams with pride. Granddad just looks a bit worried. I promise to get his book for him and Mum and I go back to the car.

Mum looks at me. "It's all a bit crazy at the moment, isn't it, Lady Boleyn."

I look at her with my eyes wide. That doesn't even cover it.

I check my phone. Lydia Portancia has e-mailed me.

> Millie! Sorry to hear about you and Danny, but your mum's vlog is genius. It opens us up to all sorts of new audiences. Please feel free to include her and Dave as much as you like. We'll all just get bigger and bigger together!
> L xxxxx

I show Mum. "Oh! Five kisses." Mum smiles. "She loves you at the moment!"

I fire an e-mail back to Lydia.

> Hello Lydia,
> I hope you understand, but I'm not really interested in trying to get bigger right now. If viral happens, it happens. My granddad's ill and I want to concentrate on him and use the vlog for fun. I'm fine where I am. I just want to enjoy it and be me. I know your other clients will keep you busy. I'll be in touch if I need any help.
> Thanks,
> Millie

I read the e-mail out to Mum and ask her if I'm a feminist warrior. Mum smiles and replies, "Millie. You are BRUTAL. You're learning. I bet she messages you back within thirty minutes."

I don't think I care if she does right now. I'm not going to fully commit myself to never caring about Lydia Portancia ever again obviously, but, at the moment, she's not high on my list. In fact, she's low on my chart of life stuff.

I don't tell Mum this, though. I'll work out a plan on my own when I'm ready. This is New Millie. I'm a mixture of "I don't care" but "I do care," and I'm giving myself time to work out what I REALLY want.

This is why I can't tell Mum. New Millie currently makes no sense, but she will after a good night's sleep and a takeout meal. There is no WAY we are cooking anything. I think Mum would get toast delivered today.

#Home

As we pull into the drive, Lauren is waiting for us at the front door. She flings herself at me as I get out of the car and starts to talk.

"Millie! Are you okay?! Are you all right? Are you okay, Mum? I mean, Millie's mum. I've been doing loads of research, and stroke victims really benefit from gentle brain activity. Oh, I told you that, didn't I? Anyway, the point is—"

Lauren forgets what her own point is. Then remembers.

"The point is THIS!"

Lauren unfurls a giant poster with a huge grin.

"THIS! This is—"

At this point, Mum interrupts her. "Lauren darling, is there any possibility we can actually get inside the house? If I don't have a cup of coffee soon, we'll need to call another ambulance."

Lauren looks at her feet. "Sorry, hospitals make me nervous. Even the thought of them."

I give Lauren a huge hug and we go inside. Mum torpedoes toward the kettle and Lauren and I head to the bedroom. Lauren is overexcited. She is flapping her hands about with her poster and it catches me in the eye. She doesn't notice, and I don't say anything as I know she's just being Lauren and trying to make me feel better.

"So, Millie, this is IT. This is how we get your pops back on track. This is . . . THE PERIODIC TABLE!"

Lauren unfurls her poster and points at random chemical elements. "We make your granddad learn a chemical element thing every day. We start simple! Ca for Calcium. Ra for Radium. And then we get harder and harder till we get to stuff that I can't even pronounce. Like, Ye . . . Ye . . ."

Lauren gives up. It says "Yttrium." I can't help her. I just nod. Lauren carries on with her speech.

"And other really hard ones like Pr, Praseodymium! I googled that one and just said it perfectly. THIS, Millie, is the perfect rehabilitation. Why are you giggling, and why are you holding your face?"

I'm holding my face because the periodic table attacked my eyeball, but I keep quiet on this front.

"Sorry, Lauren," I say. "It's a great idea. I think I'm just laughing with relief and possibly hysterical tiredness. It's all been a bit manic, hasn't it?"

Lauren nods. "Yep! Your life has been like gymnastics on a roller coaster."

I sigh. "That's why I basically just told Lydia Portancia to get lost."

Lauren goes very quiet. I think she must be in shock. Her silence worries me, so I try to reassure her.

"It's not that bad, Lauren. There are other people who can help me. Do I even need people like her, anyway?"

Lauren looks up. "Sorry, Millie, I was just thinking if it's even possible to do a somersault on a ride at Six Flags, and I've decided it's definitely not unless you want to die."

257

Planet Lauren means I have to repeat my news.

"I've sent a bit of an abrupt e-mail to Lydia Portancia."

"Oh, GOOD!" Lauren shouts. "You went viral without her. Yes, she set up the Canada thing, but I bet your mum could have done that! And she wouldn't take a percentage off you either. It would all go to college. Or clothes."

Lauren winks at me. This has made me feel a lot better. Not the possibility of an increased wardrobe budget, but the fact that Lauren thinks that—

At this point my phone dings. It's an e-mail from Lydia.

> Hello Millie,
> If there's anything I can do to help, please, PLEASE get in touch.
> Lydia xxxxxxx

Lauren makes her smug face. "Two pleases and SEVEN kisses. Who needs who, Millie?! That's what you have to ask yourself. Treat them mean and keep them keen."

"You totally got that off MUM, Lauren. That's what she says about how you should treat boys."

Lauren does a proud, wiggly walk all over the bedroom. "It works in many situations, my friend, as I have just proved!"

The way Lauren was talking, you would think SHE had written the e-mail in the first place. I go to make this point when I hear the doorbell. Lauren gets to the window first.

She pulls her "I've got some scandalous gossip" face and whispers as loud as a shout, "IT'S BRADLEY AND HIS DOG!!"

I try to act cool.

"So?" I actually DO whisper, "He's JUST a friend."

"Yeah, yeah, yeah," Lauren says with a laugh. "You keep telling yourself that. Anyway, I'm going to help your mum make instant coffee."

Lauren does a mad cackle and leaves my bedroom just as Bradley is coming up the stairs. Mum has already let him in. As Lauren passes him, she says, "Hi, Bradley! Hi, Dog!"

Lauren is not good with names sometimes. Bradley does not even acknowledge her. He won't be happy that Huevos has just been referred to as "Dog." I see him grimacing, but then, as soon as he sees me, this stops.

"Hello, Millie," he says, smiling. "I've brought you something."

#AllTheLovelyCarbs

"I got you a sandwich," he says quietly. **"You can forget to** eat at times like this. Is your granddad okay?"

"Yeah," I reply. "He's going to be all right, I think. We've got to look after him and get him back to normal. He already wants me to bring his book of flags. Lauren has come up with a comprehensive trivia plan. That sort of thing."

Bradley stares at me. "Perhaps she could start her trivia plans with the names of pets."

This makes me laugh. It's typical Bradley dryness, but this time things feel a bit different. It's the first time we've been together in a while. I think we might have moved on emotionally without even seeing each other. I know that potentially makes me sound crazy, but that's what it's like.

There's a big pause after I stop giggling, though. A big fat pause. I say the first thing that comes into my head.

"What's in the sandwich?"

Bradley lifts it up to his face as if to remind himself.

"Er. Cheese. Mayo. I think I put a bit of sundried tomato in it just for a change."

I still can't think of anything too clever, so the engine in my brain goes into spoon gear and some nonsense coughs out of my mouth.

"I'm glad you didn't put onion in it, because of, you know, the breath thing."

Bradley AND Huevos look at me strangely. "What breath thing?"

I'm really floundering now.

"You know, when I was going to see Lydia Portancia for the first time I had onion breath, and meeting new people is hard with bad breath, isn't it? You can't speak to them or kiss them or . . ."

Bradley is starting to shuffle about nervously. Huevos has given up completely and has gone to sleep in his arms. I find sleeping things quite calming, and all of a sudden the sensible part of my mind kicks in.

"Bradley. Would you like to go to the movies sometime this week?"

Bradley grins and Huevos opens one eye. It's like he's a canine psychic.

"It depends," Bradley replies. "I can do superheroes, but which one is crucial. I think most scary things are ridiculous, and—"

I interrupt him. There's been too much of this. "Bradley. Would you like to go to the movies this week?"

"Yes!" he mumbles in a good way.

My feminist powerhouse takes control.

"There's just something I want to do. Can you go downstairs and wait?"

Bradley shrugs. "Yep. Got nothing better to do. I'll google what's on at the movies."

Huevos growls. "No, you can't come," Bradley tells him. "Not after last time."

Even though I desperately want to know what happens when you take a Staffordshire-Chihuahua cross to a movie, I have something more important to do.

#Symbiosis

I walk downstairs with Bradley and find Mum in the
kitchen. She's drinking a very large coffee and Lauren is explaining the
periodic table to her. Mum knows every chemical element ever—even
the unpronounceable ones. However, because Mum is a big believer in
building female ego and self-confidence, she is letting Lauren talk. And
talk.

I can see Mum wants to escape, and I want to borrow her skills. This
is a perfect time for some social symbiosis. I learned it in science. It's
when two things can benefit each other. Or something. I get Mum away
from Lauren and she helps me with my next plan.

"Lauren, I just need to borrow Mum. Perhaps you can . . ."

Lauren spots Huevos and interrupts. "Give that a walk!"

Bradley snarls like a very unfriendly dog and says, "His name is
Huevos!"

"Yes, Bradley," Lauren says quizzically. "Why did you name a dog
after a food? Doesn't he get confused? I mean, you wouldn't call a dog
'Sausage.' Or perhaps you would. You do get . . ."

While Lauren is talking at Bradley, I give Mum the sign for "Can I see you in my room, please?" and point to the ceiling. She knows. It's a mother and daughter thing.

As we are climbing the stairs, I tell Mum my idea. She nods cautiously but smiles. This idea is a bit of a good one.

No, Millie. Own it. This idea IS a good one. That's not my mum talking. That's me.

#Mvlog

Mum and I sit in my favorite vlog spot and I press RECORD.

Hello! It's Millie.

And I'm Hashtag Help Millie's Mum! That is a title that I am allowing for the purposes of this vlog. Normally it's Ms., or my real name.

Thank you for the reaction to the thing my mum did. My boyfriend and I have split up and I was gutted, BUT since then a lot of stuff has happened. My granddad has had a stroke. He's fine, but it's made me think about what REALLY matters, and that's—

There's a burst of fur from the left. Dave tackles the phone and everything stops.

Mum and I start giggling. We can't control ourselves. Dave stares at us like we are human maniacs who she is the boss of.

Basically, it's fantastic. It sums me up. Family. Cats. Chaos. That is ME.

And I think I'm going to upload it just like that and let everyone else decide what they think is important to them.

Acknowledgments

Thanks to all the usual suspects but particularly Jo-Anne & Michael Green. Jo—there's hot water at my house for you forever.